DEATHLY TOUCH

C. C. SOLOMON

CatDog Publications

ACKNOWLEDGMENTS

Thank you to all my friends and family who supported my dreams. Thank you to my line editor, Judi, for your insight. To Ashley, Sasha, Shandril, Janete, and Tyler thank you for beta reading and giving me such helpful feedback. Thank you to my editors at Real Indie Authors, your eyesight is always appreciated. Thank you to my proofreaders at Yours Truly Book Services for catching what my eyes could not. And thanks to my readers for keeping me going. Your enthusiasm and feedback have made a huge difference.

FOREWORD

To find information on prior books by C.C. Solomon, insider extras, and a FREE copy of Mystic Bonds, Paranormal World, Book One by C.C. Solomon, go to www. ccsolomon.com and subscribe to her newsletter!

CHAPTER 1

*J*azmine St. Clair was nine when she killed her father.

It had been summer time. She hadn't been angry at the time she killed him, just scared.

Very scared.

Not of her father but of the world. The earth and everything on it, from humans to animals to even the plant-life. Everything had changed in almost the blink of an eye. To this day, she didn't understand the cause of the world changing. No one understood why the supernatural had taken over and changed so many people and things into paranormal beings. All Jazmine knew was that this magical apocalypse had changed her life forever.

The day the magic arrived had been sweltering hot, which she preferred over the cold even though the heat did awful things to her long, thick hair. The ends of her ponytail stuck to her sweaty neck, so she'd been constantly fanning herself with the hair.

However, that wasn't the point of her recollection. She was in line with her father at their favorite pizza shop, picking up their Friday night pizza special, Meatlover's Delight.

They'd left her mother and her fourteen-year-old sister, Paige, at home that July evening. She'd liked just hanging out with her father alone. They first went and got ice cream and talked about her week at school and the latest scary movie they were going to sneak and see. Scary movies used to be her favorite before that day. Before the world actually *became* scary.

Things were still normal when they'd arrived at Joe's Pizza Shop. It'd been busy that Friday as usual.

Her father looked down at her and grinned, the corners of his deep brown eyes crinkling. "Remember," he said, pointing a finger at her. "Don't tell your mom we ate ice cream. She'd be mad we had dessert before dinner."

Jazmine mimed zipping her lips shut, beaming up at him.

A scream had pierced the air, followed by several more.

Jazmine had jumped, looking behind her. The noise had come from outside the shop.

Several customers had raced past them in excitement, blocking the windows to observe the source of the commotion. The patrons closest to the windows and doors gasped.

Her father had pushed her behind him. "What's going on?" he'd shouted to the crowd in the front.

"There's something on the street," said a teenage boy, looking back at them briefly with terrified eyes before turning back to the window. "It's the plants. They're spreading all down the street."

"What?" Her father had looked down at her and had put a hand up to stop her from moving forward. "Stay here."

Jazmine had waited patiently, standing on her tippy toes to get a glimpse of what was going on, but it was no use. She'd been too short.

A paralyzing wave had washed over her, stopping her breath. She'd dropped to her knees and pushed her hands onto the cold tile floor, struggling to breathe. She remembered her heart beating impossibly loud in her little ears, and then, just as soon as the consuming pressure had washed over her, her body had slowly regained life.

Her father had raced back to her. "We need to go, now. What are you doing on the floor?" He'd reached out a hand to help her up.

She'd looked up at him, her eyes blinking rapidly as if seeing everything around her for the first time. She grabbed his hand, and her father pulled her up, then paused. He'd looked down at her with wide eyes, before letting go and grabbing his neck. He'd opened his mouth as if to speak, but no words came out -- only the haunting sound of his gurgling. Thick black liquid had poured from his eyes, nose, and mouth, and he'd stumbled backwards before dropping to the floor.

"Dad! Dad," Jazmine had screamed, grabbing his arm as he writhed on the floor, arching his back.

His eyes hadn't looked to her, and they'd clouded over in a white film.

It was a face she'd never forget, the last living image of her father.

And then he was gone.

Jazmine had continued to scream. She'd listened for his heartbeat and had shoved at his body, willing him to awaken. But his face had remained frozen in horror, his body unmoving.

Plant-life burst through the windows. Vines wrapped around some of the patrons. Others had run, screaming. Jazmine hadn't been able to focus on any of that then. All she'd been able to see was her dead father.

A woman had grabbed Jazmine's arm. "Come on. I'm sorry, honey, you can't help him. We've got to go." The woman had quickly let go to stumble back. And just like her father, this woman had spewed black liquid before collapsing, dead.

3

Jazmine had remained on the ground, staring between her dead father and the dead woman in shock.

Ten years into the new world and Jazmine still suffered from the pain of that day. The memories were still so vivid, the sound of her father struggling to breathe as his insides had liquified, his face filled with confused terror.

Terror that she'd put there.

The memory of that night jarred her awake many nights. Jazmine hated sleeping. That's where the nightmares resided. Instead, she often stayed up late, playing video games and watching old movies. However, it didn't matter how late she finally slumbered, the memories haunted her in her dreams.

Jazmine stood on her small balcony and breathed in the late spring air, shaking off the heaviness of that day like a cold chill. However, the air was still heavy with heat. It was technically spring, but in this new world, there were really only two temperature seasons -- winter and summer. One day it would be forty degrees, and the next it would be eighty or higher and stay that way for six months before dropping to twenty degrees in the snap of her fingers.

She took a sip of her tea and looked down at the quiet street. It was still early morning on a Friday. The streets would be silent for a while, just as she liked it. She could go out without the looks of fear from other people.

Six years ago, Jazmine and Paige had found this community in the northern part of Virginia not far outside of D.C. Now known as New Hope, the town spanned over five square miles and was like many towns in the country since the supernatural apocalypse, self-governing. Recently, there'd been a push for the reemergence of the defunct federal government, which had crumbled during the early years of the paranormal apocalypse and the following pandemic, often called the Sickness. Several communities across the country were now controlled by a collective of government representatives called governors who independently ran their towns but were collectively joined like a federation. New Hope was one of those government-controlled towns. It was the safest and most stable residence Jazmine had lived in since before the world had become magical, or the Pre-World, as they called it.

She heard a knock at the door and sighed, walking back inside her apartment toward her front door. She didn't get that many visitors. Mostly just her controlling sister from time to time to nag her or complain about the way she lived her life.

She looked through the peephole. Theodore "Theo" Alverez stood on her doormat rocking on his toes.

She opened the door and let him in, giving him an unceremonious 'hey' as she closed it behind him.

"What an enthusiastic greeting," Theo exclaimed, before rifling through her kitchen cabinet near the entrance.

Jazmine leaned against the counter beside him and placed her hands on her hips. "What are you doing?"

"I ran out of cereal, so I figured you'd have some," he replied, pulling a container down. He looked at it and brought it to his chest. "I used to hate this cereal when I was a kid, but the fact that they are making it again gives me all sorts of memories. One of the good things about living in a government town, easy access to processed foods."

Jazmine shook her head and grinned as she watched her friend grab milk from the refrigerator and a bowl and spoon. Theo was her *only* friend. He had been since she'd first came to town. After all, he was one of the few people, besides her sister due to her healing magic, who could touch her.

Theo was a zombie. Actually, zombie was not the politically correct term for him. He was the reanimated or undead. Although the paranormal happening validated a lot of the horror films and stories that Jazmine had come to know, one myth that was wrong was that the undead just randomly came to life and go around as mindless shells, eating brains and infecting more people. The undead could not typically be raised without the power of a necromancer. Most of them weren't super intelligent, and many would only have a limited life span, depending on the strength of magic from the necromancer.

Theo was one of the rare undead who had risen on his own. He'd been alive when the magic had arrived and hadn't even realized what he was until years later, when he was killed by a vampire. He'd awakened moments later but not as a vampire. Instead, he'd returned as a being who craved human brains and flesh, much like a ghoul. By eating human flesh periodically, he regenerated and his intelligence was maintained, so he didn't become the zombie of old horror movies. Oddly enough, he also aged, albeit slowly like all paranormals, and ate human food.

Most naturally animated undead looked just like a regular human, and aside from the whole brain eating, hard-to-kill, superhuman-strength bit, he was a regular human. He was average height with a wide grin and friendly hazel eyes against lightly tanned skin. His jet-black hair was cut shorter on the sides and longer on top. He was handsome, in a boy-next-door sort of way, and with his large eyes, he had instantly put her at ease when they met in school. Outside of his tattoo-covered arms, which he'd only acquired in the more recent years, after his mother had stopped threatening to disown him, he didn't look like he would hurt a fly.

Most importantly for Jazmine, since he was dead already, he didn't die from her touch. He was safe.

"What's the game plan for tomorrow?" he asked, before eating a mouthful of cereal at the counter.

Jazmine tapped her chin and squinted. "Hmm, walk to the couch and play some video games. Walk to the balcony and read a book. Walk to the bedroom and take a nap."

Theo nodded thoughtfully. "Sounds exciting. Instead of playing those life simulation games—"

"I play a lot of fighting games too."

Theo gave her a thumbs up and a fake smile that wasn't meant to be encouraging. "Hear me out. We go to a bazaar. There's a good one at the Wharf in D.C. It's not far."

"No, thank you. I'm quite happy at home."

She stayed in a one-bedroom apartment a floor down from her sister in one of the many high rises in the city. She was only nineteen, and under normal circumstances, she'd be living with her sister. Except Paige was engaged to Bryant Montgomery, a telekinetic who was also the deputy governor of New Hope. Jazmine was sure that Bryant wasn't a big fan of hers, so she moved out on her own.

She didn't need anyone. It was better to be alone. Saved a lot of lives. Saved a lot of heartache. People were usually irrational and harmful. They never understood her, whispered behind her back, called her names. She'd tried to socialize from a distance, but no one had wanted to put in the effort towards talking to her, and the few encounters she had she was so awkward, she feared she'd never know how to carry on a decent conversation.

No, it was better for her emotional well-being to stay away from others and to just focus on surviving. She did her job, creating online content and games of all sorts from educational to recreational. The internet was the number one source of entertainment now anyway. All channels on TVs were provided through streaming services. As long as a community had a witch or a tech mage to provide electricity and technology – which had stopped upon the return of magic—they would never go off the grid. And since most of Jazmine's time was spent alone, video games and the internet were her main sources of activity.

Working in entertainment wasn't as lucrative as it once was since medical, building, teaching and magic skills were the most desired. Still, she made a comfortable living in her town where capitalism was becoming king again. In other non-government communities, credits, services, and bartering were still the primary resources for survival. Jazmine's job was becoming more profitable as the years went by, but she just wanted enough money to build her online presence and keep to herself.

Theo put his bowl down and pointed his spoon at her. "How? How can you be happy? For the six years I've known you, all you do is walk circles around your apartment all day. First your sister's, now this one."

Jazmine put up a finger. "One, I do work." She put up another finger. "Two, I do go for walks at night after most people are off the street. I also go to the store early in the morning."

Theo rolled his eyes. "Yes, yes. How exciting. You're nineteen. The drinking age in town is now eighteen, and you're a paranormal. You could live another two hundred years. Is this how you want to spend it? In a cramped apartment eating sugary cereal?"

Jazmine sucked her teeth. "Thanks for the judgement. Maybe I'll move into a cabin in the woods by a lake and grow a garden. Get a little canoe and go on the water. Watch the sun set and rise each day. Read all the books. I really don't have a need for people. They just get weird around me, and I then I don't understand them, and then it becomes a whole thing." Even as she said it out loud, she knew how pathetic it sounded.

Theo gave her a pitying look. "Aw, no. You need to live. You have the gloves. You're safe."

Most people knew about her magic touch. She'd had to announce it for the safety of others when they'd arrived in town. She'd only been thirteen, yet had still been isolated and treated like a leper at school. She'd sat in a classroom with other "undesirable" students all day and had watched lessons via a screen.

Even three years later, when a local witch had developed

special gloves to prevent her from killing those she touched, people still feared her. They didn't trust the gloves, and everyone knew she could still kill with other parts of her exposed skin and through any non-magical material covering her. And, therefore, from the last hug she'd received from her father at the age of nine until her current age of nineteen, she had not felt the touch of another person, except her sister, who only hugged her on rare occasions. Those hugs were usually weak. She waved her gloved arms in the air. "These things only go a little past my elbows. That's not keeping people safe if they bump into me, and wearing the magic hazmat suit all the time is stifling in the summer."

Theo shrugged. "Other people at the bazaar wear hazmat suits. Scared humans who still aren't sure if they're immune to the Sickness and scared paranormals who don't want to catch this new paranormal disease out there."

In what could only be seen as cosmic revenge, there was now an illness that was infecting paranormals. Unlike the Sickness, which only affected regular humans by destroying their organs and senses, the paranormal illness made one go insane and violent. No one was sure how it transmitted. Some believed it was via bodily fluids. Others believed it was actually a bad drug reaction that had become contagious. There was now a test for it, but it wasn't easily obtainable yet. Not that Jazmine was worried about catching anything with her self-imposed isolation.

She wondered if the undead could transmit disease. She gave Theo a suspicious look.

But he was oblivious to her concerns. "Go in a bikini under the hazmat suit. It'll be cooler that way. And then, if you see a cute a guy you can zip it off and flash him."

Jazmine gave him a blank stare. "I don't understand why we're friends."

Theo chuckled before picking his bowl back up. "We're friends because I'm fabulous and you're fabulous, but other people are too stupid to know it. You *cannot* waste your hot years hiding in your apartment. Get yourself a man."

Jazmine nodded slowly. "Right, and then kill him. Because that is what would happen if I touched another person. I haven't encountered any other self-raising undead besides you yet. And all the other kind of undead are a no-go."

Theo tapped his chest lightly. "Yes, yes. I am taken. However, there are others almost as great as me out there. In fact, someone showed me a new app. It started as a way for vampires to find donors but also has a dating track. You can meet guys all over the world. If you have access to teleportation magic, it's easy. Maybe you can find someone with your type of magic in some fabulous city like Paris."

Jazmine sighed. "A dating app? Isn't that what they had years ago? Sounds depressing. Scrolling for love. Not very organic. Although practical, I suppose, if used correctly."

"Yep, I was only ten when the world went to crap, but my young Aunt Christina used to be on all of the apps. She met all sorts of guys. I remember my mom calling her fast, but she was young. She was living. What else do you do?"

Jazmine shrugged but didn't speak. A dating app seemed well beyond her social abilities. She'd been so used to self-isolating that she had zero flirting ability. What would she talk about? What would she wear on a date? What if she never met anyone who wanted to risk having her touch them? Right now, she had a vague hope, but if she got on an app and got no interest from men all over the world, well, that would be down-right depressing.

"What about undead vampires?" Theo asked, taking another bite of cereal. "I heard there is a hot one in Silver Spring."

Jazmine shook her head vigorously. "Undead vamps go bloodlust too easily. Plus, they don't want to risk touching me either. They aren't sure if I'll kill them. Honestly, I still don't understand why *you* touched me."

Theo waved a hand at her as if shooing her away. "Honestly, I tripped over my shoelace, but it all worked out because I *am* dead. How can you make me any deader?"

Jazmine pointed a finger at him. "Fair point."

"You're going to the bazaar with me," Theo stated, putting the finished bowl in the sink.

Jazmine stomped a foot. "Can't you ask Matt to go with you?"

Theo grimaced at her. "You know he can't move during the day. Even that magic serum he takes from time to time only works for a limited time. Plus, shopping's not his thing."

Matt, Theo's live-in boyfriend, was a gargoyle and turned to stone during the day.

Jazmine huffed. "I don't like shopping either."

Theo dropped his shoulders and pouted. "I risked my life by touching you, and *this* is how you repay me?"

Jazmine's eyes widened. "Wow. You're using guilt now? Before, it was 'no big deal,' now it was a 'life-threatening' event." She pointed an index finger at him. "Fine. What time is this spectacular bazaar?"

He threw his hands in the air. "It starts at seven. And no worries. We'll take the necessary precautions so you don't get touched," Theo replied before heading to the front door.

"Seven? Wait. What? That's night. Matt could go with you."

"No, no. He's busy, and it doesn't get dark until after eight now. I'll be here by six-thirty tomorrow. Try to comb your hair and put on something other than sweatpants or tights. Maybe a sundress," he called behind him before leaving.

Jazmine frowned and looked down at herself. "Sundress?" She didn't even think she owned one. She looked around her apartment, a slight panic washing over her. She hadn't left town since she first moved in. The thought of going to some crowded market at night where anyone could bump into her and die sounded like an awful idea.

She already had enough to atone for by killing her father and the innocent woman. A day didn't go by where she didn't think of them and remember their horror-filled faces. Not that her sister ever let her forget anyway. She was a danger to society and had killed a father she loved dearly. Now Jazmine was agreeing to put lives in danger to do a little shopping? What kind of precaution would Theo be able to come up with that could stop her from killing people?

CHAPTER 2

*E*van Kitagawa poured dark red liquid into several shot glasses before passing them to the small gathering of men and women at the bar. They were celebrating something he cared too little about to hear. They were part of the town's elite, the hunting force.

They weren't farmers or hunters who killed animals for their meat. They did hunt, but it wasn't for deer or duck. It was for humans. Sometimes, they made deals and exchanges, many times they just took. Evan was part of a town full of vampires, after all. Sure, they mostly ate food, but the substance that allowed them to live was blood, and human blood was best.

Travis Parker grabbed several of the shot glasses off the bar and passed them to those around him. He turned back to Evan and gave a sharp-toothed grin. "Kitagawa! Take a shot with us. On me."

Evan picked up the extra shot on the counter and lifted it towards Travis with a curt nod. He drank it back, fighting back a grimace from the bitter liquid. They'd asked for a strong blood type and whiskey shot. The blood had come from a large male, and it carried its own full-bodied, earthy taste. Before he'd become a vampire, he would have never have imagined that blood could differ in taste depending on the type of person or blood type. Being a bartender for the last couple of years, he'd learned otherwise.

Travis laughed at him, his hazel green eyes crinkling. "Not a fan, huh? You know you'd be able to handle the stronger stuff if you'd grow a pair and come hunting with us instead of serving drinks behind the safety of this counter."

The people around him chuckled, giving Evan scornful looks.

This wasn't a new conversation. Every time Travis saw Evan, he had to pick a fight. When he'd first tried to recruit Evan to the hunter force, Evan had politely declined. He wasn't afraid of fighting. He wasn't afraid of much these days. But hunting wasn't his interest. He wished he didn't need blood at all.

He preferred to keep his head down low. He'd managed through these past ten years since the world had changed by sticking to himself. Before he'd been forced into coming to the vampire town, he'd spent his years living off the grid with what remained of his family, until he'd come across this vampire community, and they'd all but forced him to join them when his last family member had died.

He'd been seventeen at the time and had been practically feral when the town leader, Jasper, had found him. He'd been living alone for almost two years then and had lost any desire to be around people. People killed just as much of his family as the Sickness. However, Jasper had convinced him to join the town and had raised him like a son even though he'd been practically an adult.

"Hey." Travis rapped the counter with his knuckles. "Earth to Kitagawa." The muscled bully waved his large, bronzed hand in front of Evan's face. "We asked for another round. Wake up."

Evan rolled his eyes, grabbed the same blood bottle and

14

then the whiskey on a lower shelf. He really hated that guy, but he needed this job until he figured out what he wanted to do with his life. He poured the drinks in the now empty shot glasses.

He looked up when he heard a loud clang. A serving tray rattled on the black tile floor surrounded by food. A short man with blue eyes and black hair looked down at the floor with a surprised frown.

"Where's our usual waitress?" shouted a large freckled man with a blond Mohawk. He was part of the hunter group who was now sitting around a large, circular table.

"Yeah, who's this guy?" added another man with long brown locks.

"Delia is out today," said the short man Evan knew as Jacob. "Why'd you trip me? This is the food you ordered."

"Replace the food. It's not our fault you're clumsy and fell," a woman with cornrows spat from across the table.

"I didn't trip on my own," Jacob insisted, balling his hands in a fist. "That guy put his foot out and tripped me." He pointed to the blond mohawk hunter.

"Are you back talking to us? Isn't the customer always right?" asked the man with brown locks as he leaned in towards Jacob. "Now clean this shit up and get us a new order. And call Delia in."

Jacob looked down at the food as if contemplating it.

"On your knees," mohawk stated, leaning back in his chair with a cocky smile.

Jacob shook his head and bent over to put the wasted food on the tray.

"Good boy," cornrows sneered.

Evan shook his head. He knew Jacob didn't just drop that tray. He had certainly been tripped. The hunters were good at what they did, but they were mostly a group of assholes. It was the main reason Evan never wanted to join them, although he was a good fighter and hunter of all things himself. He knew they were just picking on Jacob because he was smaller and weaker than them. Half the reason Delia didn't come in that day was because she was tired of their harassment and groping, and they didn't even tip well.

"Problem, Kitagawa?" Travis asked with a wide grin.

Evan wanted to wipe it off of his face. He knew it wasn't genuine. Travis used his smile to disarm and confuse people, but Evan was never confused. He knew it was a mask, and he would never let his guard down around him or waste valuable time wondering why Travis behaved the way he did. Travis was a bully. They all were. They were stronger. They were supposed to protect others.

That's not what the hunters were about in this town, and Evan had little patience for it.

Evan crossed his arms. "Yeah, I have a problem. Your pal over there tripped Jacob and wasted our food. They don't have to be dicks about him cleaning it up either. If they want to get off on tormenting people, they can do it somewhere else. And Delia isn't coming in today just to deal with your bullshit."

Travis nodded, still keeping his grin. "I don't see how you keep a job. You're lucky you're Jasper's adopted son." He shook his head. "I don't know what he sees in you."

"Maybe that I'm not an asshole," Evan muttered, before grabbing a glass to clean.

"What'd you say?"

"You heard just fine. You're a vampire. You've got great hearing."

Travis reached over and shoved Evan in the chest, making him drop the glass and stumble back, catching himself before he slammed into the row of liquors behind him.

Evan should have kept his mouth shut. He knew it, but he couldn't help himself. He really hated Travis. Evan sucked in a deep breath, although he really didn't need to since he was dead. He looked over to Travis with an unreadable face before his mind went blank.

He lunged over the counter and slammed Travis's head into the bar before jumping back with his hands up in fake surrender. "Shove me again, Parker," he said through gritted teeth.

Travis stood up and touched his lip. His grin widened when he saw the blood on his fingers. "You know, I knew you were stupid but not that stupid."

Evan shrugged. He'd fought Travis before. He knew how the hunter fought. He was often technical, fighting as if his movements came from instructions in a manual. It didn't mean it would be an easy fight. The instruction manual was quite dense, and Travis had been built for combat.

Travis was average height with his light brown hair cut close to his scalp. Some called him a pretty boy, but he wasn't a suave ladies' man. He was a soldier meant to harm, except the harm rarely touched his youthful face. Of course, as a vampire, he aged at a snail's pace and healed in the blink of an eye.

Evan was taller than him but leaner, although still toned. Even though he got in a ton of fights when he'd first arrived to town, he never looked like a fighter. He was a brooder, as his few friends called him, with tousled jet-black hair and eyes so deep brown they almost looked black. When he wasn't working at the bar, he was home, reading. He wasn't an extreme introvert, but if the owner of the bar wasn't his friend, he'd be back in the woods, jobless but happy.

Evan let out a deep sigh. "Is this where you punch me to teach me a lesson? And we fight...again?" Evan looked behind Travis at his growing crew of hunters closing in on them.

Jacob cleared the floor and ran to the back.

Travis narrowed his eyes and sneered. "What's wrong with you, man? We can all kick your ass in here."

Evan looked around the small, dark bar. It was only moderately busy, and he was certain no one was going to jump in the fight besides Travis' crew. They'd seen this show play out before, and there would be nothing they'd win by attacking the leader's son.

"I don't need any help kicking your ass myself," Evan shot back. He stuck out his chin and leaned forward. "Come on. I'll let you get your revenge hit."

Travis lost his smile and grabbed Evan by the throat, drawing his fist back. "You smug, motherfucker." He dug his nails into Evan's throat, drawing blood.

"No fighting in my establishment." shouted a voice behind him. "He's on duty. Let it go."

Evan turned slightly to the bar owner, Lamar King, or King as everyone called him.

He walked behind the bar counter from the direction of his office. King was older. He looked late thirties or early forties, but he could have been sixty for all Evan knew. He had short, curly black hair with a bit of gray in it and a black mustache and goatee. He had friendly brown eyes and a lazy smile set against rich brown skin. Even while annoyed, he still held an approachable disposition. It was a true sign of maturity and wisdom that he had been trying to instill on Evan.

"Tell your employee to stop picking fights then," Travis shouted, pointing at Evan.

King nodded. "And I'd say you do the same. This next round of drinks is on me," he replied, pouring another round in the small group's shot glasses.

The hunters grumbled but took the drinks.

When he was done, he tilted his head to the right, directing Evan down to the farther end of the bar. "Son, how many times have we talked about this?" he asked, placing a hand on Evan's shoulder.

Evan nodded. "I know, I know. The customer is always right."

King chuckled and shook his head. "No, they aren't, but if we want to stay in business, we have to at least make them like coming here. Being a smart alec won't get them to stay."

"He is always testing me," Evan grumbled, crossing his arms.

"He's a bully. We get it. Let that shit go. You're an adult now. You're twenty-one, and you have a long life to live. There are much bigger things to deal with than his mouth. He only says that shit to get under your skin, and you fall for it every time."

Evan shrugged. "This is why I just need to go back in the woods and be alone. I can't deal with these people."

"Son, you can't just run and hide because you're having a tough time dealing with something."

Evan narrowed his eyes. He didn't agree. He never did. He was doing just fine on his own. "Why?"

King sighed and shoved his hands in the pockets of his jeans. "Because you're human. Yeah, I get that you're a paranormal. But don't let that mean that you can't still be who you were born to be. Don't let being a vampire be an excuse to go run and shut down. Even Jasper wouldn't want that."

King wasn't a big fan of the town leader, Evan could tell. However, out of respect for Evan and his job, King never said much about him.

King tilted his head and lifted a brow in a curious glare. "You been listening to those meditation audiobooks I sent you?"

Evan rolled his eyes. "Yes. They're ridiculous."

King patted his shoulder and chuckled. "I know, I know. But give it some more time. You're a good kid. I don't want you shutting yourself down. You got a lot to offer this world. Jasper clearly knew it, or he wouldn't have adopted you at your age. He could have just brought you to town and sent you on your own since you were practically an adult or put you in the kid's home with the rest of the kids who lost their parents, but he took you in instead. Don't let him down by giving up on yourself. He's got plans for you, and it ain't working forever in this bar."

Evan sighed and slumped over the bar as if he could no longer hold up his own weight. He knew his adopted father wanted him to do more in life than just be a bartender, but Evan enjoyed the work. Jasper didn't need to focus so much attention on Evan. He was just letting Evan have his fun for now, and he could barely stomach the idea when Jasper would finally come calling for him to do whatever he had planned.

King tapped his chin before putting his hands on his waist. "Tomorrow, I have a job for you. You're going to the night bazaar. Pick up a few things for the bar. I'll give you a list. But have some fun with your friends. Drink a little, eat a little, listen to some live music. Have fun."

Evan squinted his eyes and scratched his head in confusion. "What is this fun you speak of? And friends? What are those?" He cracked a smile.

King laughed before pointing a finger at him. "Don't act simple. I'm giving you a night off on my dime. Take it, and don't ask questions."

"I just want to stay working here."

"Well, son, if you keep being rude to the customers, I don't know how long that'll be." King winked before walking up to the counter to take another drink request.

Evan knew he was right, but he just couldn't help himself. It wasn't that he hated people. He just hated the challenges that some of them caused. He just wanted peace. He just wanted happiness. He was 21, but he still missed that eleven-year-old kid he used to be who played baseball and video games with his friends. The kid whose only worry in life was getting opening night tickets to see his favorite science fiction movie.

He touched his chest. Now his biggest worry was if he'd ever have a heartbeat again.

~

*E*van flung himself onto his bed when he got home at five in the morning from the bar. He turned his head and looked out the floor to ceiling window of his high-rise apartment. The light of dawn slowly crept its way through the cracks between his closed blinds.

He lived in a city far from his prior life. Vampires had taken over many major cities across the globe. This community resided in D.C. near the water. It had taken him a long time to get used to his new environment. He'd half hoped his brother would be there, but it seemed he'd gone to another town to start his life over.

Evan would have preferred going to a city not so close to the water. After all, it was water that killed him. He'd drowned in the lake near his cabin. He'd been a great swimmer, so it wasn't due to his own clumsiness or a leg cramp. No, a gigantic, tentacled creature had decided to take up residence, or rather make a sudden appearance, in the lake at the precise time Evan had been going for a swim. It had wrapped its tentacles around Even's body and had squeezed the life out of him while holding him underwater until he'd died. Just for fun, apparently, because the creature hadn't eaten him. And when Evan had awakened under water, he hadn't been the same.

As a non-living vampire, his heart could no longer beat, and he could barely eat or stand the sun. He also could not have kids. It seemed this line of the Kitagawas would die out. He was too young to think about kids, but the thought of never having them did sadden him a bit.

His life had seemed to be one misfortune after another until Jasper had found him. For the past five years, he'd lived a fairly untragic life, and it was just the way he liked it. He didn't need adventure or fighting or love. He just wanted to survive and live his life day by day.

However, as was his usual luck, the fates had something very different in mind for him.

CHAPTER 3

*J*azmine looked through the peephole of her apartment door the next day and sucked her teeth. Whenever her sister came by, she always had to prepare herself for some form of disapproval. Her sister seemed displeased with most aspects of Jazmine's life.

Paige greeted her with a stern face as soon as the door opened. She moved past Jazmine and walked in, carrying a cotton tote in her hand. "I went to the store this morning. I'm assuming you didn't," she said in a clipped tone as she put the tote of groceries on Jazmine's kitchen counter.

"No. I think I'm good today. Plus, I'm supposed to be going to some night market thing with Theo tonight so I could have gotten food from there." Jazmine leaned against the wall as she watched her sister take out the contents of the bag and put them away.

They were all healthy or essential things. Fruits, vegetables, bread, eggs, meat. Nothing fun. Didn't her sister know that potato chips and jelly beans were being made again? Not even any chocolate chip cookies were in there. Jazmine sighed internally. Eating this way explained why Paige was so trim and why Jazmine, who would go back to the market to get her processed goodies, had a little more padding around her center.

While Jazmine had a power that could kill, Paige had developed a magical touch that could heal. It made perfect sense it would work out that way. They had always been polar opposites. Paige was tall and athletic, having been on the volleyball team. She kept her black hair no longer than bob length with beautiful curls that framed her high cheekbones and honey colored eyes.

Jazmine was barely average height with a curvier frame. She kept her thick, black hair long. She envied her sister's slim face and light eyes against her own round face and dark brown eyes.

Paige had been a popular kid in middle school. She'd even been popular as a freshman in high school.

Jazmine had been a bookworm in elementary school, and her only extracurricular activity was the drama club in which she'd helped build the sets. And that was only the one year in fourth grade. After that, there wasn't any school for a while.

Paige paused before putting a small bag of apples in the crisper and abruptly stood up straight. "You're going out?" she asked, spinning around. "Tonight?"

Jazmine nodded, looking away. She already knew by her sister's alarmed face that this was not going to be a fun conversation. "Theo's forcing me to go."

Paige put her hands on her slender hips. "He cannot *force* you to go anywhere."

Jazmine poked her lower lip out. "I don't know, Paige. He's a zombie. He's pretty strong."

"You know what I mean. You need to stay here. It's safer."

"Theo says I can take precautions. He just called to tell me he has some temporary magic stencil I can put on that acts like a bubble or a ward so no one can touch me."

Paige huffed. "I've never heard of anything like that."

Jazmine rolled her eyes and adjusted in her stance. "It's new. You don't know everything."

"And what if this stencil thing is a hoax? Someone bumps into you and then dies? Do you want to kill another innocent person just because you want to have a little fun? They could lock you up or worse."

Jazmine grimaced and looked down at her feet. Her mind drifted to her father. The memory of what she'd done washed over her again, and she left the small walk-in kitchen to sit on her couch.

Paige followed her. "I'm not saying this to hurt you. I just want what's best for you."

Jazmine knew what Paige thought best for her. She wanted Jazmine to stay in her bubble, going no farther than the apartment on most days, until she died. But she didn't want to live like that forever. She didn't want to never love anyone. She wrapped her arms around herself. She missed touch.

She looked up at Paige. "If the stencils work, can't I go? Just for a little bit?" Jazmine hadn't been excited about the idea earlier, but after thinking about it, the thought of experiencing something new became more and more appealing. Her exile for life was slowly killing her, even though she tried her best to ignore it.

Paige rubbed her forehead, closing her eyes. "Don't think that I'm not out there trying to find a cure for you. You think I enjoy you spending your days, years in here?"

Jazmine shrugged and looked out of the window.

"If you think I'm such a monster, then why would have I taken care of you all this time? With your...personality, you weren't always easy. I just want to make sure this experience doesn't make things worse for you. I really don't have the time to pick up the pieces if you get hurt. And if you killed someone, it will ruin us."

Jazmine huffed and leaned her head back on the couch. "I'm not an idiot. I wouldn't hurt anyone. I know better now."

Paige refused to look impressed. "It's not just about you. There are other worries out there. I've been treating folks who've fought against people out there trying to steal paranormals for their blood."

Jazmine sat up. "Yeah, I heard about them on the news. Some human group kidnapping paranormals to make some sort of power serum."

Paige shook her head. "It's not just them. I heard it could be vampires swiping us as well. Paranormal blood is pretty potent. And people always want to attack government town citizens. They want to see the government fail and not come back."

The world seemed on the cusp of change again, and not everyone liked that. There wasn't a president for all the government communities yet, although people were beginning to campaign for the big election next year. Once a president was elected, Jazmine knew the next focus would be what to do about all of the towns who refused to rejoin the government.

"Are you listening to me?" Paige cried. "That bazaar gets all types, and the government helps to sponsor it, so it's a target. What if someone tries to kidnap you?"

Jazmine looked up at her. "Have there been attacks there before?"

Paige glared down at her. "No, but it's at night, and a lot of dangerous things can happen at night. It's only a matter of time. It may not even be vampires. It could be worse, dark fairies. The Fae are scary. They might whisk you away to their realm, and you'll never be heard from again. Is that what you want?"

Jazmine shrugged. "If they don't die when I touch them, maybe it won't be so bad." Sensing her sister's rising anger at her joke, she quickly spoke again. "It's only a matter of time that any bad thing can happen. The world changed on pizza night. I could wake up tomorrow and shoot lasers out my eyes. That could literally happen. I saw on the news the other night how a girl told her teacher that a gremlin ate her homework, and it was true. It was her pet. People have gremlins for pets now." Jazmine threw her hands out to the side. "Really? What kind of parents does she have?"

Paige dug her hand through her straightened hair. "You've been cooped up in here too long. Maybe you should get out, but not to the bazaar. Go for a walk or something. And," she said, changing the topic slightly, "I saw that news report as well. They were a family of ghouls, so I think having a gremlin for a pet is fine for them."

"Oh." Jazmine scratched her neck in thought. "I still want to go to the bazaar. If just for one night, can I live like a real person? Just one night!" She clasped her hands in front of her face, as if begging her sister.

Paige rubbed her temples clearly at her limits with Jazmine. "I absolutely just cannot deal with you. Fine, if you get attacked or kill someone, don't come crying to me."

And with that, her sister stormed out of the apartment, leaving Jazmine open-mouthed and stunned.

∾

"*I* don't understand why I had to get so dressed up to basically go to the store," Jazmine grumbled as she looked out of the passenger side window of Theo's car that evening. She smoothed out some wrinkles on her yellow spaghetti-strapped a-line dress, feeling overly dressed. Her long hair hung in thick curls around her shoulders. To top off her look, she'd applied only a fuchsia lipstick and some black mascara from the town's only beauty store.

Theo shook his head as he drove them in his red hybrid sports car. "Because it's a social event. The few times you see

27

people, you should try to look your best. It's not rocket science. You know, it's a real tragedy you've never gone to the bazaar before. It started off small a couple years ago, but then just grew and grew. It's more than just a market. You'll see."

Jazmine nodded absentmindedly and looked down at her wrists, both displaying spirally circle stencils. She'd practiced touching plants and had even chanced touching a bird before she could be convinced she was protected. Nothing had died. She hoped this also worked on people because she wasn't about to test-drive that. She'd put her elbow-length gloves back on as an added precaution. She'd also put on a magic infused jean jacket. If anyone bumped into her, at least she'd be covered from skin to skin contact. Thicker clothing material like jeans usually worked as a protective barrier. Now she had to hope no one touched any other part of her exposed body. Maybe she should have worn the hazmat suit.

They drove on, quietly listening to music play in the car before arriving to what Jazmine could only describe as a carnival of lights, sounds, smells and activity. People were everywhere, walking around several booths filled with goods of all sorts and lit with strings of lights. Clothes, food, jewelry, services, artwork, books, and antiques filled the various rows of booths. Several stages were strategically placed for bands to play, and there were picnic tables for people to eat. There was even a DJ area, and groups of people danced carefree under magical orbs of floating light. A thrilling wave of exhilaration passed over Jazmine as she spun around, looking at her surroundings.

Theo put a hand on her shoulder. "I need for you to stop twirling around like a country bumpkin seeing the big city for the first time. Please, and thank you."

Jazmine rolled her eyes. "Fine. But this is kind of major. I mean, look at all the clothes they're selling. If I cared about dressing up, I'd be in heaven."

Theo snorted. "I wish you cared about clothes as much as you do your hair. You're practically Rapunzel with all that hair, but I can't get you out of sweats and muumuus."

Jazmine stopped walking and turned to him with serious eyes. "I have never worn a muumuu."

Theo threw up his hands and hunched his shoulders in surrender. "Fine, large shapeless dresses that everyone *else* calls a muumuu. I mean, you go to bed in it sometimes."

Jazmine shrugged. He was right. Fashion wasn't her thing. When the world had changed, fashion had fallen to the bottom of her kid priorities.

Theo led her around the bazaar, which she was beginning to think was an incorrect name for something so festive. They bought food and sipped drinks as they strolled, listening to the various musicians as they browsed over items. They used their government dollars to purchase items, although she saw others, not part of government-run towns, barter instead.

When they weren't browsing for items to buy, Theo tried to get her to flirt with boys. She shyly looked away if she caught a guy's attention, definitely not ready for that. She could barely have a regular conversation with someone without sounding like an awkward freak.

Someone brushed against her back, and she jumped forward, instant panic seizing her heart. God, she hoped the stencils worked. She spun around, wide-eyed.

"Sorry," said a tanned man with wavy black hair. He had high cheek bones and lips so full Jazmine forgot herself and zoned her gaze on his pout, momentarily wondering what they might feel like. She wasn't sure she'd ever seen someone so handsome in person before. He was tall and broad-shouldered and looked like a model. He was way out of her league. Why did she care about leagues? He was a stranger.

He gave her a slight smile with a head tilt forward in apology before walking on.

Jazmine nodded and put a hand to her chest to calm her racing heart. She wasn't sure if it was beating so fast because she'd almost killed someone or because he was so cute. Maybe it was both.

Theo gave her a calming rub on her back. "It's okay. See, nothing happened. He just touched your jacket. By the way, he is too damn cute. Too bad he's with someone."

Jazmine twisted her lips as she looked on at the woman standing next to the guy. "You have a boyfriend."

"I wasn't talking about for me."

Jazmine rolled her eyes. "I need another drink. My nerves are shot." She turned away and then stopped as loud screams filled the air.

~

*E*van crouched on the ground in front of a booth full of dresses wishing he could be anywhere else but there with his adopted sister and her girlfriends. This was not how he wanted to spend his Saturday evening. He'd rather be working.

"This dress would look gorgeous on me," Thalia MacNamara exclaimed, putting a short polka-dotted dress to her chest.

"So cute!" exclaimed her blond-haired friend.

"What do you think, Evan?" asked the other woman, a short brunette with freckles. She lightly tapped him with her foot.

Evan released a deep sigh and turned away. "Someone, kill me now."

When he'd agreed to hop a ride with his adopted sister and her friends to the bazaar, he'd regretted it as soon as he got in the car. He was going to have to find his own way back. He'd run. He was a vampire, after all. It wouldn't take him long. He'd put the bags of liquor in the car and could get them out tomorrow.

Thalia pouted her red painted lips and flipped her long, red hair over her shoulder. "Aww, you're no fun, Evie."

He cringed inside. How he hated that nickname. However, he tried his best to hold in his annoyance. She was the leader's biological daughter, after all. An eighteen-year-old spoiled brat but also his adopted sister. "What time were you thinking of leaving?"

"The night's still young. The market doesn't close until two in the morning," said the blond, batting her eyelashes at him.

He swore. He wasn't sure how much longer he'd be able to put up with these girls. He gulped down the strongest cocktail he could find as the women paid for their outfits. When they left the booth to head to another, they suddenly stopped and screamed in unison as they rushed forward to hear a band they'd been waiting to see.

Startled, Evan almost knocked a woman over. She turned to him with surprised eyes, and he apologized before Thalia yanked him away by the wrist. He looked back at the woman with curious eyes as she spoke to what he assumed was her boyfriend.

She was beautiful, with a cloud of long, thick hair and large brown eyes that he could only describe as doe-eyed. It was as if he could fall into the depths of them and get lost. She had satiny cinnamon colored skin complemented by a fitted yellow dress that clung nicely to her curves. She was beautiful but odd. Why was she wearing gloves and a jacket? It was almost ninety degrees out. *Eh,* he thought, *a place like this* would *cater to weirdos.*

"Come on, Evie," Thalia shouted.

He hung his head and turned back to the group of women, wondering if it would be rude to just disappear.

They didn't really need him. He was just in the way of them flirting.

Several screams suddenly interrupted his internal pity party.

Crowds of people ran in various directions from some unseen predator.

Were they under attack? Was it a beast or other paranormals?

"Vampires," screamed one woman, picking up her child and magically teleporting away.

"What?" Thalia cried. "There are already vampires here."

"They must be bloodlust," her blonde friend guessed.

Evan pushed the girls to the side as the direction of the crowd veered their way. He had to see what chased them.

Several beings dressed head to toe in black with only red eyes peering out of ski masks materialized in an open space within the crowd. One being, most likely a man based on the frame, grabbed a screaming woman by the arm. She struggled against his tight grasp but it was futile. As quickly as the man had appeared, he disappeared, this time taking the woman with him.

Evan focused his attention around him as he thought of their next move. He saw more of the black-clothed beings grabbing attendees and disappearing with them within the crowd. There was no hiding when these people were just appearing and disappearing in a blink of an eye.

Evan turned to Thalia. "We have to get to the car."

She covered her mouth, shaking her head. "Where's Natalie?" She looked around, holding her packages close to her.

"They took her," her brunette friend yelled hysterically. "They took her!"

"We have to find her!"

Evan shook his head. "We don't have time. Let's get to the car. Run as fast as you can."

The women looked at him with wide eyes, frozen in place.

"Now, damn it!" Evan growled.

The trio immediately took off, running past slower running attendees. To the naked eye, a running vampire looked like a blur of colors. They were simply too fast. He wasn't sure what these beings were, but he was banking on them not being fast enough to grab a vampire in mid-run.

Once they arrived at the car, he opened the driver's door and shoved Thalia inside.

She struggled against him. "I'm not leaving my friend!"

Evan grabbed Thalia by the shoulders. "Get out of here. I'll look for your friend."

Thalia looked up at him with dazed, horrified eyes. "We can't leave without you."

Evan relaxed his shoulders and gave her a reassuring smile. "Don't worry about me and don't wait for me. I'll get back to town. But if they've taken her, there's nothing more we can do without our hunter force. Both of you get out of here. I know how to take care of myself."

"Watch yourself," she shouted, getting in the car with her friend who was already crying hysterically in the front passenger seat.

"Always," he called, backing away from the car.

She peeled out of the grassy lot, almost running over a screaming teenager.

Evan sucked in a breath and headed back to the chaos. What was he supposed to do? He wasn't Superman. He could very well get snatched up too. But he *was* a vampire and an undead one at that. What would they be able to do with him? His blood was basically poison to anyone.

Maybe he'd have to get himself caught in order to find Thalia's friend. He ran through the bazaar entrance, bumping against running patrons as they exited. Since the attendees were rushing out, the area was getting cleared, so it was easier to see the kidnappers in the wide-open space.

He caught sight of a male attacker in black reaching out for an older man who had jumped backwards out of the way. Evan tossed the man aside, waving the older patron away. The man in black raced towards Evan, tackling him to the ground and pounding Evan in the face and body with a barrage of punches at lightning speed.

Evan lowered his arm from protecting his face and quickly grabbed a knife from his pocket, stabbing the man in the neck with full force. The attacker jumped up and stumbled back, yanking the knife from his neck and pressing his hand against the bloody wound.

Seizing the moment, Evan jumped up and kicked the attacker in the chest, sending the man onto the ground. Unfortunately, the man regained his composure quickly, his neck wound already healing, and propelled himself in the air towards Evan. But he was ready for him and stabbed the man in the chest with his knife upon the attacker's landing. The man fell to the ground, taking Evan with him.

Evan shoved the man off him before pinning him down with his knee. "Where are you taking these people, you fucker?" he shouted, pressing his knee into the now groaning man's chest. Evan wiggled the dagger when the man didn't speak, causing the attacker to cry out but still remain mum. He tore the black mask off the man and raised his eyebrows in surprise as he saw long pointed incisors.

Vampire.

The teeth, coupled with the blood-red eyes, were the main signs. No other creature had two fangs of that size along with red eyes with just a small black pupil in the center. But this man was not bloodlusting. He didn't have the other indicators such as ashen, almost marble-like skin, pointed ears, and bald head.

He saw many of the attackers teleporting. They couldn't

all be vampires then. Teleportation wasn't a gift vampires were supposed to have. They had incredible speed, the ability to jump impossibly high and flight, but not teleportation. What was going on?

Evan took out another dagger from his sock and stabbed the man in the thigh, eliciting another shout of pain. He kept multiple knives on him. It was a habit from living in the middle of nowhere in an apocalyptic world.

The man shouted in pain but still did not speak.

"Okay. You like to play it the hard way, I see." Evan dug his knee harder into the man's chest as he reached in his other back pocket for another knife.

He looked up quickly to ensure no surprise attacks and suddenly stumbled forward. He quickly looked down in surprise.

The man was gone, and so were his daggers. Luckily not Evan's favorites.

"What the—" He jumped up. The man had vanished into thin air in just a blink of an eye.

A blinding pain erupted from his chest, and he looked down in shock as he saw a bloodied hand protrude through his stomach. His mouth filled with his own blood, and he stumbled forward, attempting to tear himself away from the owner of the fist. He spun around and swung his knife, but the masked man from earlier teleported away again.

Evan should have been overcome by his injury, but he barely felt the pain. He was an undead vampire. As long as the injury didn't destroy his non-beating heart, he could survive. Or so he hoped. He was admittedly feeling a little woozy already.

Hairs prickled on his arms, and instinct immediately took hold of him. He spun around and stuck his knife out, connecting with the masked man who reappeared in front of him. He quickly swung the knife upwards and headed towards the heart.

The man shook and began to fade out in an attempt to teleport. However, the injury Evan had given him was too severe, and he was apparently having challenges.

Taking the opportunity to stop the attacker, Evan forced his other hand into the man's chest and ripped out his heart. He crushed it in his hand and grimaced at the man. "If you're going to a punch a hole through someone, aim for the heart."

The vampire, succumbing to his injuries, dropped to the ground.

Evan tossed the smushed heart over his shoulder and grasped his stomach. The gaping wound was large and angry. Maybe he would enter his final death from this injury after all. He looked around the area for help. The space was almost empty, save for a few injured people. The attack seemed to be over, and he'd failed to find Thalia's friend or learn much of anything helpful really.

He wasn't sure he could get home in his condition. He needed to rest. Actually, he needed blood to help speed up any healing and then sleep. If he could just walk out of there and find an animal, that would be a start.

He turned to exit the venue, having given up his search of Thalia's friend in favor of trying to live and met a small fist to the eye. He stumbled back, grabbing his right eye and grimacing at the person in front of him. "What the hell?"

Wait, he knew her. Well, he didn't really know her. He'd seen her before.

The pretty woman with the long hair and yellow dress looked over to him with a wild expression. She took a step forward, raising her fist again. "Back off, mother fucker!"

He took a careful step back, lowering his hand as the throbbing pain in his eye quickly subsided. "Relax," he began but then hunched forward, grabbing his chest.

Why did his chest hurt now? His heart was constricting. No. It was burning. He rubbed the heel of his palm into his chest as if his organ could feel the pressure and relax.

However, the constricting ignored his futile attempts, and his heart remained in a vice grip until suddenly it left.

"What the hell was that?" he wondered out loud, still hunched forward with a hand still on his stomach.

"What?" asked the woman with confused eyes.

"What is right, lady. I—" he stopped mid sentenced and frowned, grabbing his chest again, only this time there wasn't pain.

No, this time, his heart was beating.

CHAPTER 4

"How are you alive?" Jazmine asked the stranger.

The man looked down at his chest then up at her again. "My heart's beating," he said in a voice deeper than she expected.

"Welcome to the human race." She tilted her head with squinted eyed confusion. "I touched you. And you're still alive."

"You punch hard, but not that hard." The man snorted. "By the way, why *did* you punch me?"

Jazmine raised an eyebrow and looked down at the gaping wound in his stomach. Not only had he managed to survive her touch, but he stood as if the hole in his body was just a minor scratch. What *was* this guy? She'd taken off her gloves and rubbed off the protective tattoos to defend herself when all hell broke loose. She hadn't wanted to actually kill anyone, but she was no fan of dying either. She'd thought he was a vampire attacker when she hit him, but maybe he was something else. How else would he have survived her touching him?

Even if it was brief, the skin to skin contact was all she needed to have her touch take hold. Heck, even touching someone through a T-shirt was enough. She figured that out when she tried to pick plants up with napkins and still killed them. That was why her gloves had to be so thick.

"I thought you were one of the bad guys since your eyes were all red. I got scared because people were disappearing. Otherwise, I wouldn't have been so quick to touch you," she answered before pointing at him. "You have a hole in your stomach. You know that, right?"

He frowned. "I look like a bad guy to you?"

"You have red eyes, your fangs are hanging out, and you're wearing all black." She looked back down to his stomach. "Seriously, does that hurt?"

He sucked in a breath and grimaced. "I was fighting an attacker just now, and my eyes do change, and my fangs drop in a fight. And you're punishing me for my fashion choices? And yes, this hurts. I have a hole in my stomach."

She squinted her eyes at him as she crossed her arms. He really didn't look like the bad guys. His black outfit was not the same as theirs, but she was running on adrenaline at the time. Crap, if he had died, she would have killed a third innocent person. The thought made her almost want to vomit.

The man swayed slightly and stumbled to remain upright. "I'm probably going to pass out soon, but you look like you might faint or throw up. I can't really tell. You going to be okay while I'm passed out?"

She shook her head quickly, not sure if he was joking, although he really didn't look well, what with the hole and all. "I'm sorry for hitting you."

He dropped his hands and gave her a soft smile. "It's okay. I've been hit worse."

"Well, the least I can do is help you. You can't pass out here. What do you need?"

The man headed to a booth and sat on top of the counter. She followed him.

"Well, a wound of this type will require me drinking

blood to heal. Think you can find a rabbit to get me?" He cracked before sucking in a breath. "Shit, this hurts."

Jazmine bit her lip and frowned. Why did she feel guilty? She hadn't ripped into his stomach like that. What if he was hurting an innocent person, and he or she was just defending themselves? However, he didn't seem like a bad guy. He hadn't fought back when she punched him in the eye.

No, she should leave him there and tell the authorities to help him. That was the smart thing to do. And yet...

She looked at him, his face scrunched in pain and covered in sweat. She could help, and he hadn't died by her touch. Maybe it was time for her to finally help someone instead of hiding away.

She pushed her wrist in front of his face. "Drink."

His frown deepened as he looked at her hand. "No."

She withdrew her hand and looked up at the night sky. Why was he being so difficult? "Aren't you dying? Do you really need to be so picky? My blood isn't poison." At least she didn't think it was. God, she hoped it wasn't. She wouldn't be able to survive killing another innocent person.

The man hung his head on his chest as if it were too heavy to lift up. "I don't want to hurt you. An animal works just fine."

Jazmine placed her hands on her hips. "Do I look like I hunt animals for a living? You'll be dead by the time I find a rabbit. I can ask someone here to help, but I don't know if they have blood on them. You'll have to wait until the medical teams start showing up to heal the injured. I don't have that kind of power."

He looked up at her, head still lowered. "What type of power *do* you have?"

"Don't worry about that. Let me help you." She shoved her wrist back in front of his face. He was already looking paler. Why was he being so stubborn?

He looked it over as if inspecting it. He gingerly touched

40

her arm before bringing it to his lips. The feel of his soft skin on hers sent a slight shock to her core she didn't expect.

And then he opened his mouth, exposing two very long incisors.

She stiffened and wondered whether she should step away. What if he bit her arm off or didn't stop sucking her blood, draining her dry? Nope, this was a dumb idea.

She was just about to move her arm back when she caught his eyes looking up at hers. He looked unsure of himself as if he really was afraid of hurting her. But there was something more in his face.

Sadness? Something in her heart softened. She knew about sadness. That kindred feeling pushed her to nod at him.

He lowered his eyes and bit into her arm.

And it hurt. Well, she knew it could. She'd heard tales of a vampire bite being pleasurable, but this was not it. It felt like she was being stuck by two large needles. Her knees weakened, and she cursed herself for not sitting down first. *You're a big girl, Jaz. Keep it together. And if he goes too far, stab him with the knife hanging out of his pocket.*

She remained strong as the man drank from her, making quiet, sucking sounds as he gently grasped her arm. The act felt so intimate. She didn't even know this guy's name. Should she have gotten it first? Would that really have mattered?

She swayed slightly and suddenly realized that the pain from his biting had disappeared and was now replaced with a pleasant tingling quickly spreading throughout her body. It felt a little inappropriate to feel this way in public. An uncontrollable shiver swept over her, and her eyes fluttered closed for a brief moment as she felt the wave of pleasure pass through her. Every part of her hummed from the top of her head to the soles of her feet. She felt like she would explode right there and then. So embarrassing. And so good.

Then the pressure from his mouth on her wrist disappeared along with its accompanying pleasure. A flood of disappointment rushed her, but she pressed her lips tight together and adjusted in her stance.

She looked back down at the man as he licked dribbles of blood from his lips. Even his act of doing that sent her stomach to tingles. *Jazmine, get it together. You are acting like a horny idiot.* Maybe she did need to join that dating site Theo suggested.

The man looked up at her, a rejuvenating shine to his eyes now. "Thank you. You taste good. And that sounds very inappropriate," he muttered, swiping a hand through his hair.

"Thank you?" she asked more than said. There she went being awkward, but he seemed awkward too, so they were even. She looked down at his stomach.

It was healing before her eyes. Vampire rejuvenation was very impressive. She'd never seen it up close before. The process of organs reforming and skin knitting together was pretty...gross.

She looked around at the vacant booths to avoid his horror show of a stomach. Security was dispersed around the area, and she knew soon other town police forces would appear. Too little too late. How did anyone fight an entity that could disappear and reappear in the blink of an eye?

"They're going to want to question us," she stated.

He nodded. "Yeah, that's usually how it goes."

A thought entered her mind, and she could have kicked herself. Theo was going to kill her. If she ever found him, that is. "I need to find my friend. We split up in all the commotion. Hopefully, he's at the car. Take care." She turned and walked away.

He called after her. "I can walk you."

She turned slightly and watched him slowly stand up like an old man. She waved her hands at him. "No need."

He looked like he needed to stay seated and rest for a while.

Her work here was done.

"I know." He touched his chest again.

What was wrong with him? Was he not feeling well? She was the wrong person to help heal anyone. She'd done the best she could. If he had a heart issue, it was beyond her.

He walked towards her, this time appearing less weak. Maybe he was getting better.

She shrugged. "Fine." He *was* cute. She didn't mind spending a bit more time with him. Plus, she really needed to find out how he had survived her touch. Only Theo and Paige had lived after touching her, and she couldn't let someone new slip by. He had a heartbeat, so he was alive. Could living vampires survive her touch? If so, that opened up a whole new world for her. At least dating-wise. Undead vampires were still rare, but living vampires were a large group in the paranormal community. She side-eyed him. Maybe she could even date him, assuming he was remotely interested.

"What's your name?" he asked, walking beside her.

Names! That's right, with all the excitement she'd forgotten to ask. "Jazmine St. Clair."

"Beautiful name."

She looked up at him. Was he flirting? He wasn't looking at her, just straight ahead, still touching his chest with a strange dazed look on his face. "What's your name?"

"Evan Kitagawa." He looked down at her and finally removed his hand from his chest, offering it to her.

She looked down at his hand as if inspecting it. Okay, she'd gotten away with punching him, and he'd drank her blood, but old habits die hard, and she had to be on the safe side. She dug in her pocket to pull out her gloves. She'd already rubbed the stencils off to fight the attackers, but she wondered if maybe some trace of them still remained. That would explain him not dying.

Evan gave her a puzzled expression and grabbed her free hand, shaking it. "I don't have anything. It's okay to shake my hand."

She looked down at their hands together for a moment in shock. His skin felt warm and soft. Was all skin this warm? God, she didn't remember. She just didn't want to let this contact go; it felt good.

She held in her disappointment when he let her go. She finished digging out her gloves with her other hand and put them on out of habit.

Evan snorted. "Too late now. You have the cooties."

"I can't touch people," she muttered before looking up at him. "How are you alive?"

"You keep asking that." He tilted his head back, gazing down at her with lazy eyes that had the effect of looking both suspicious and sexy. "What's the deal?"

She shook her head as they exited the bazaar. "Doesn't matter."

"Matters to me."

She lifted a shoulder. She really didn't want to get into her death touch right now. "Where is his car?" Jazmine sighed and squinted as she searched the lot. Most of the cars were gone now, and she was sure they had parked in the front of the bazaar.

"Your boyfriend's?"

Jazmine clasped her hands together, trying to control her growing fear. "Who? No, he's not my boyfriend. Well, he's a boy that is a friend. So, in a way, he is my boyfriend."

Evan rubbed his chin as he studied her, a confused expression on his face. "What kind of car is it?"

"A red sports car."

Evan nodded slowly, searching over the cars on the grassy field, which served as the lot. "Nope. Don't see that."

Jazmine side eyed him. "Thank you for confirming with your man eyes. Apparently, my little female ones don't work well."

Evan smiled again.

Why was this guy always smiling? And he had the nerve to have dimples in both cheeks. *Ugh, so cute.* No, she would not be distracted by this stranger she'd never see again.

"How are you going to get home? Magic?" he inquired, eyes narrowing.

"I don't have that kind of magic. I don't suppose your car's still here?"

"Nah, I sent my friends home."

She turned to him and scrunched her face. "Why would you do that?"

"So, they can be safe. We lost a person in our group, and I said I'd find them. Clearly, they aren't here. Mostly likely kidnapped." He pressed his lips together and frowned in concern.

"Sorry to hear that." Jazmine crossed her arms, feeling suddenly very fearful. She was practically alone in the night with a stranger. If Theo's car wasn't there, then she'd have to face the fact that he'd left her. That jerk. If he wasn't immune to her touch, she would have strangled him. No, she wouldn't, that would mean killing him. Damn it, she wanted to kick his ass. He was cut from being her friend, as if she had friends to lose.

What the hell was she going to do? She'd never felt so alone before. Scratch that. She'd felt this alone. Ten years ago, when she'd had to walk home from the pizza shop in the dark, scared from the supernatural dangers of the night and pained by the death of her father. She shivered, although there was barely a cool breeze that night and tightened her hold on her arms.

"Do you live close by?" Evan asked, peering down at her with a concerned face.

"In a car, I'm under twenty minutes away."

"So, not that close to be walking."

"What about you? Never mind, you're a vampire. You can just race where ever in the blink of an eye."

"Vampires do get tired. And I live pretty far from here. Like Philly far."

She raised an eyebrow. "You came all this way just to go shopping?"

He threw his hands out to the side. "This bazaar is a big thing. You had to have seen that before the chaos."

She rubbed her forehead in a sad attempt to gain some idea of her next move. "I guess I can see that." She looked around again. More police forces were arriving. "Well, I'm sure we can get security to take us back to my area. I can drive you home."

"Aren't you tired? By the time all this settles down, it'll be late before we get to your town. And then driving me to Philly from around here is probably about three hours one way. And I live in a vampire community so I doubt you'd want to spend the night, especially after all this."

"No," she said quickly, leaning back from him. "No offense. You seem nice." She let out a breath. "Well, if I don't drive you tonight, you'd have to stay in the area. I'm from a government town, and you getting in this time of night and not being affiliated with another government town is probably not likely."

He gave a quick shrug. "It's not a problem. I can go to a nearby hotel and catch the first train headed north. You can come with and call your friend and curse them out while they pick you up." He smiled again, and her heart did an annoying twisty thing.

She nodded. "There's a hotel about a mile and a half from here."

"Great, well, then let's go." He held his elbow out for her arm to link through.

She walked forward. What did he think this was some romance novel from long ago? However, she needed to draw the line. Better not to set her up for that sadness. "I'm not touching you again. And we have to talk to security first. Then we go."

"Fair enough," he said, raising his hands in surrender.

~

*E*van didn't like lying. He couldn't recall the last time in his life that he'd ever told a lie. He'd been an annoyingly good kid and a responsible adult. Well, except for the fighting. But assholes like Travis really deserved it.

He really hated lying to Jazmine by telling her he lived so far away. It was just that he knew if they separated now, he'd never see her again. He had to know how she'd gotten his heart to beat. It was still beating strong in his chest.

And he could breathe!

He'd forgotten to notice that part. He was so used to breathing as a force of habit before, but he actually *needed* to now. He could feel the difference.

He looked over at her as they walked silently down the dark main road, having left the bazaar after answering pointless questions from security. The road was framed by abandoned houses and cars that lacked the magic ability to get running. Abandoned sections of the world were common. He couldn't wait until there was a concerted effort to clean up the forgotten neighborhoods and streets. Travel would be so much quicker and less creepy.

Sure, he was a vampire, but that didn't mean he wasn't nervous about some crazed werewolf or giant troll popping out of the bushes. He'd fight them to the death either way, but it wasn't his preferred activity.

As he looked at Jazmine, he wondered if she was scared of walking in the dark. With him. He was a stranger, and yet, he didn't want to be. He felt connected to this woman now. She had given him life, and she had no idea. She was his freaking hero.

He was already in her debt from letting him drink her blood, which was the best thing he'd ever tasted in life, and he wouldn't mind another opportunity to taste her. However, her jump-starting his heart made him even more gracious.

"Why do you keep staring at me," she asked, her eyes forward. "Just because you have that vampire night vision thing going for you doesn't mean I can't feel your eyes boring into the side of my face."

"Sorry." He turned away. Then slowly looked back at her. "Why do you wear those gloves? It's hot as hell out."

"How are you—"

"Please don't ask me how I'm alive again. It hurts my feelings. Do you want me dead or something?"

She let out a snort, and the soft laugh tickled his ears with delight.

He liked the sound and wanted to hear more of it.

"These gloves are to protect me from hurting people. I— I...kill people when I touch them. That's my Midas touch. Except I don't turn things into gold."

"Actually, when King Midas was touching people, they weren't exactly living as gold statutes, so it's not too far off." He pointed at her. "Did you just roll your eyes at me?"

"It's really not fair that you can see me in the dark."

He shrugged. "Perks of being a vampire."

"So, you're a living vampire. Well, that *is* interesting because, in theory, my touch should have killed you. I mean, I even kill plants."

He wasn't sure he believed her, although she didn't seem like a liar. But a touch that killed people? How had he survived? More importantly, how had she made his heart beat?

48

"Maybe you don't fully understand your powers?"

He heard her sigh, and then she knelt to the ground, taking off one of her gloves to touch a patch of grass next to the sidewalk. The grass withered and died in the low light.

"I'm not a child. I've been living with this for ten years. I've killed people. Yet, I touch you, and you still live to talk to me. Why is that? The only beings I can touch are zombies and my sister."

Evan scratched his head, perplexed. "I wish I knew why but I guess I should tell you that when I first arrived at the bazaar, I was not a living vampire. I was undead."

Jazmine stood up and turned towards him with wide eyes. "*Now* you tell me?" She threw her hands in the air. "Well, no wonder I didn't kill you with my touch. I mean—wait, but didn't you say your heart was beating?"

Evan nodded his head vigorously. He grabbed her hand and brought it to his chest.

Her eyes widened briefly.

This was an intimate action. He moved his hand, but hers remained, which made him happy. "You touched me, and my heart started beating. I started breathing. I haven't felt my heart beat in six years. I feel like a new man. A real man."

Jazmine lifted an eyebrow with a smirk, moving away. "I made you into a real boy? Like Pinocchio? Am I your blue fairy?"

He wanted to pull her back. "I think you just might be. In all seriousness, how'd you jumpstart my heart?"

Jazmine shrugged and started walking again. "No clue. That's not my ability. I don't bring things back from the dead. I send them to death. My ex-best friend is a zombie."

Evan poked his lips out in thought. "A zombie? That's like being best friends with your dog."

"Uh, if you say that to him, he really will bite you. He's one of the few that are self-aware and fully functions like a normal human...for the most part."

"Ah, I've heard about that kind on the internet. So, you don't know how you did this? Well, maybe that's your thing, bringing dead things back to life. Except zombies."

She nodded as they started to walk again, but she didn't seem that impressed with herself. He was way more excited than she was, which made sense, being that he was the one affected by this. "I don't think you're seeing the full scope of this. You can make a business of this. It's better than necromancy because you aren't making someone a zombie. You're bringing them fully back to life."

"I really don't know why this happened. I don't want to start charging people for it. This could just be a weird one-off."

"Well, whatever it is, I'll take it." He reached out and grabbed her hand again. He wasn't sure if he was holding her hand for his sake or hers, but he liked the contact. "Thank you."

She looked down at their hands, but he couldn't read her expression. He supposed she was still not used to the touching. He couldn't imagine going ten years without really touching anyone. Had she even had sex before? She did have this guy friend, Theo. Maybe she wasn't so lonely. Yet, by the way that she kept looking at their hands together and....was that a squeeze? Yes, that was definitely a squeeze. She was enjoying this interaction.

He squeezed her hand back. He certainly didn't mind holding her hand. Here they were going on an evening stroll, hand in hand under the stars and the moon, and she was absolutely beautiful. He wasn't much of a romantic, but he couldn't ignore this setting. Even with the weird gloves on, he liked holding her hand, but it would be better without them.

"Can you take your gloves off? We've already established you're not going to hurt me, and I think it's a good idea that we hold hands since we're walking in the dark. I don't want anything snatching you away."

She giggled and took off one of her gloves, putting it in her pocket.

They kept holding hands and talking, making it to the hotel without any incident other than having to jump back as some werefox ran past them.

The hotel was a former three-star chain that was filled with cars in the lot. They were most likely for those attending the bazaar. He hadn't lied when he said it was popular and people came from afar. Every month for one Saturday during the summer season, it was always grander than normal, so it pulled a lot of people.

While he bartered to get the last room in the hotel, Jazmine called her friend.

Evan didn't want to say goodbye yet, and the frown on her face hopefully meant she felt the same. "Is your friend picking you up?"

Jazmine let out a dramatic sigh. "No. He said his car wasn't there when he got to the lot. He thought I left him. He ended up catching a ride with someone he knew from town. Said his car must have been stolen. So, I have a little problem." She looked to him with a sweet, nervous smile. "He can't get to a working car tonight, and apparently no one will want the killing-touch girl sitting in their car, so he has to get a new one to replace his old one."

Evan frowned. People wouldn't even sit in the same car she'd been sitting in, and all he wanted to do was touch her again. People were crazy.

"I could call my sister, but she warned me about coming to this in the first place, and I really don't want to hear about it. I asked Theo to tell her I was safe and not to worry. So, in conclusion, can I stay here over night? I can sleep on the floor. I suppose you won't kill me since we did just walk through dark, quiet streets for the past half hour."

Of course, she could stay the night with him. He was already getting depressed about her having to leave, so this extended time was like a gift. "Absolutely," he replied a little too eagerly for his comfort. He cleared his throat. "And you can sleep on the bed. Sleeping on the floor is good for my back."

She smiled and gave him a curt nod. "Thank you."

They quickly got to his room and entered the small space. It was basic with one king bed. Technically they both could sleep on it and not even touch, but he didn't want to make her uncomfortable.

Upon entering, she immediately went to the bed and laid down after kicking off her shoes.

Evan raised his eyebrows and scratched his head. Was that it? No staying up all night and talking to each other about their hopes and dreams? Who was this woman? He had to know. Clearly, she wasn't that into him. Perhaps he misjudged the handholding. Maybe she was just happy to have any human contact, and she wasn't too particular about who it was from.

Dejected, he lay down on the floor near the foot of the bed. He was wide awake; he thrived at night, after all. How could he sleep with her so close?

Soft fabric brushed his forehead. He looked up and saw a pillow and Jazmine's face hovering over the edge of the bed. She smiled at him again, and perhaps he heard angelic bells, he wasn't sure. Wow, what was wrong with him?

"You need a pillow," she said matter-of-factly.

"Thanks," he said, taking the pillow. "So, are you sleepy?"

She shrugged. "A little."

Silence.

"Did you want to talk some more?" she asked in a quiet voice.

He nodded swiftly.

"What about?"

Everything. "Where were you when the world changed?" he asked, looking up at her.

She frowned. "At a pizza shop with my dad. He...didn't make it. So, I had to go home alone."

He shook his head, although he knew she couldn't see him. They'd all lost so much when magic came, and he could easily relate to the fear she must have had at the time.

"When my mom and sister went back to the shop to find my dad, they didn't believe he was dead. The place was already covered with those man-eating plants. But my mom was desperate. She ran to the shop, and a vine snapped out and grabbed her. It lifted her in the air and threw her on the roof of the building where she was devoured by the rest of the plant-life. I was able to touch the plants and stop them from getting my sister, but it was too late for my mom."

Evan gave a hard swallow. He could only imagine how horrifying it had to have been to witness both parents dying. So many survivors were orphans now, but the nightmares of this world came differently to people.

"Interestingly enough," she continued, her voice strong, in spite of her words, "that was how I found out that I could kill not only people but plants and animals and even food growing from the ground and trees."

He wanted to get up and hold her, but he wasn't sure she'd appreciate it. He was still a stranger to her. Honestly, he couldn't understand this desire to hold her so much. He wasn't a mushy guy. If he liked a girl, he'd tell her she was cute, they'd make out, maybe even hook up, and that was it. He didn't have crushes, and he didn't date. Was he really just mistaking any interest with her romantically to really being curious about her power? Well, it didn't matter. He wouldn't see her after tonight. However, he could still be considerate. "Jazmine, I'm—"

He heard her shift in the bed. "What about you? What's your story?"

He sighed. This was not the small talk he was hoping for, but he supposed it was only fair to swap such tales. "When the world changed, I was coming home from my softball game with my family. I lived with my parents, grandparents and my older twin brothers. I felt a change happen to me, like I was momentarily paralyzed, but no powers showed up. For weeks we all just stayed in the house, only going out for food. Then one day, one of the twins and my dad went out, but only the twin came back. Apparently, my dad was killed by a werebear. Then my other brother and grandmother died of the Sickness."

The Sickness was the real horror of the world. As if it wasn't bad enough that magic and the supernatural had taken over in one night, an illness had soon followed that had killed half the population, leaving mostly those turned into paranormals and a lower population of humans without magic. It was like the world was trying to renew itself into its current magical form with technology only existing through the power of more magic.

Evan sighed again and closed his eyes, replaying those days in his mind's eye. "After that, we packed up and relocated to a remote cabin in Virginia where we stayed for a while, growing and hunting for our own food. Things weren't great, but nowhere was in those early days. Then my granddad died." He paused, shaking his head at the memory and opening his eyes. "And then he came back the next night. As an undead vampire. I don't know when he could have drank blood when he was living for that to happen. It didn't work out though, because he went into bloodlust, and my brother had to kill him. Then my brother became a vampire and left to go to a more populated area."

"Didn't you want to go with him?" Jazmine asked, peaking down at him.

He nodded. "Yeah, I wanted to keep an eye on him so he didn't go bloodlust too. But my mom was too scared. I had to stay with her. I think my family's magic is that we can become vampires upon death with no other aid, like how your friend became a zombie. My mom thought that made us dangerous, but my brother didn't care. And after all that loss, my mother didn't survive much longer. She died in her sleep. She didn't rise. Then I lived alone for a while after that."

"So, you know all about isolation."

"Yup, I actually liked it. The few people we'd encountered weren't so good. You really aren't missing out on much. Look what happens on your night out."

She snorted, and he found even that cute. "Let's talk about something lighter," she suggested.

He wracked his brain. He wanted to talk to her about any and everything. He just wanted to stay awake with her and hear her talk all night. "What was your favorite show as a kid?"

She laughed, and he instantly smiled. He couldn't remember smiling this much in years, and he would remember this feeling. If only for one night, he'd felt really alive in more ways than one.

CHAPTER 5

*J*azmine awoke to the sound of the telephone ringing. It took her a moment to gather her surroundings. She'd momentarily forgotten what she was doing in a hotel and quickly looked down at Evan, sleeping soundly on the floor. He hadn't even budged at the ringing. He was even cute sleeping. She wanted to touch him: his hair, face, chest.

The persistent phone knocked her back to attention, and she scrambled to answer it. The front desk informed her that a guest by the name of Theo was waiting downstairs for her.

She hung up and sighed. She knew she'd have to leave, but it bothered her more than she wanted to admit. Well, it was just one night of talking and holding hands. It might not have seemed like much to the average person, but to her, it was the best night she'd had in a long time.

Even being able to share the stories of their pasts made her feel better. She'd cherish the memory and move on. She wouldn't be sad. Now she had hope. Undead vampires were immune to her touch and maybe even living vampires. There was a community out there that she could be a part of. Maybe a life of isolation wasn't her only way.

She got out of the bed and put her shoes on, feeling renewed. She made up the bed because it felt distasteful not to and decided to leave her email address on a notepad by the phone just in case he should ever want to keep in touch.

Jazmine looked down at Evan and waved. "Bye. It was really nice spending this time together," she said to his sleeping form. "Should I wake him?" She shook her head in response to her own question. "He's a vampire, and he's dead to the world right now."

She gnawed at her bottom lip. She still wasn't ready to leave. She bent down and stroked his hair lightly, a slight smile on her lips. His hair felt like silk. She bet he never had a bad hair day. She paused, mid-stroke and frowned. She probably looked like a psycho right now. Petting him like some cat. She looked around the room as if searching for hidden cameras.

"Okay, woman, get a move on before crazy Theo comes in here making a fuss." She straightened up and gave one long last look at Evan before turning and leaving.

When she exited the hotel, she found Theo in a green SUV in the driveway. "What took so long?" he grumbled, looking down at his watch.

"Really? Mr. Leave-A-Best-Friend-Behind?" she asked, opening the passenger side door and jumping in.

Theo winced as he started the car. "Sorry one thousand times, lady. You're going to hold this over me for a while, aren't you?"

Jazmine leaned back in the seat and crossed her arms. "Of course."

Theo drove out onto the main road heading towards their town. He gave her a worried, quick sideways glance. "How was your PG one-night stand?"

Jazmine rolled her eyes. "Please don't call it that, and it was fine."

"Look, I know you haven't been out in the world much, but there is still such a thing as stranger danger, kiddo."

"He didn't hurt me. He was trying to save people," she replied, resting her head on the window.

"You lucked out. I know I told you to meet guys but baby steps."

"It wasn't like that. Like I said earlier, we just talked all night. He stayed on the floor. It was nice to talk to someone new besides just via the internet."

"I can't believe you talked all night. You barely talk to anyone just for the heck of it."

Jazmine shrugged. "That's because it's a waste of time. Once they find out about my power, they rush off. Anyway, he seemed like he really needed someone to talk to, so it's the least I could do for almost killing him." Truth was, she enjoyed talking to Evan. He was surprisingly easy to talk to, but she wouldn't tell Theo that. He'd make a big deal of it, and she honestly didn't even think she'd see the guy again. Although he did ask if he could visit her one day, and she had said yes. Still, she didn't really think she'd see him again.

"So, tell me more about this almost killing him thing? On the phone, you said you touched him, he didn't die because he's an undead vampire and you somehow got his heart to beat again?"

She nodded. "I might have a new power."

Theo tilted his head from side to side in thought. "What if he's lying? What if he just said all that to get close to a pretty girl. Guys can be creeps."

That thought hadn't escaped her. She wasn't as naïve as some thought. Still, if he was telling the truth, she couldn't ignore the implications. "If he's lying, then he would be dead. There are only two options. He was dead, and I got his heart to beat. Or two, he was alive and survived me touching him. Either way, it's not normal. And either way, he survived my touch."

Theo let out a breath. "Maybe you always had this power, and he helped bring it out. Or maybe he's just a guy who can withstand your touch. Looks like your friendship circle just widened."

~

*W*hen Evan opened his eyes, the first thing he did was jump up and look at the bed. He knew Jazmine would be gone, but his heart still sank to see the empty sheets. She'd even pulled the covers back in place, so it looked like no one had slept there at all. The only give-away was a notepad in the center of the bedspread with some writing. He picked it up and smiled. She'd left her email address for him to contact her.

No, he wasn't supposed to care. He hadn't even gotten to make out with her. He wasn't going to go out of his way to find this girl. She was just another girl.

Even as he thought it, he knew how silly it sounded. Jazmine was not just another girl. She was no flighty, super-ficial vampire like Thalia and her friends. She was smart, funny, and she'd helped him without asking for anything in return.

He really was off right now. He wasn't looking for a rela-tionship. He didn't even know how to date. He wasn't sure he could repay Jazmine for what she'd done for him, but he would find a way, even if she didn't ask for it. He wanted to do something for her.

He looked down and touched his chest, then frowned. He put two fingers to his wrist. Nothing. He pressed the side of his neck. Still nothing.

His heartbeat was gone.

He looked around the room in confusion as if the answers could be found in the small space. Dropping his shoulders, he hung his head. He had to talk to Jazmine. He needed some answers, and he needed to see her. Did she stop his heart? That would make no sense. They'd gotten along so well.

Before he could search for answers, he had to get back to town. He had purposely not called home last night, and he was sure a few people might be worried. The sun was setting now, so it was safe for him to be out.

It took him no time to run back to his town, and the first thing he did was go to Jasper's house.

Thalia cursed him out sufficiently, upset that he hadn't returned the night before and had not found her friend. Evan allowed himself to be screamed at, and when it seemed Thalia was running out of steam, the pair headed further into the house to find Jasper.

As expected, the leader of the town was busy in his study, surrounded by a few of his council members discussing the prior night's attack. When Evan and Thalia walked in, Jasper looked over to the others in the room and tilted his head to the door. "Let's break for dinner and reconvene in an hour," he said in a calm tone.

The small group scurried out of the room, giving nods to Thalia and Evan as they departed.

"Glad to see you're alive, son," Jasper stated, crossing his fingers together and resting his chin on his hands. "Is there any reason why you did not come home with your sister last night?" The older vampire's eyes betrayed no anger, only curiosity.

Evan rarely saw Jasper get angry. In fact, it was his pleasant disposition that made him so endearing to the people. Well that, and the fact that he was a dictator who had no problem with disposing of his enemies and those who broke the rules with a ruthlessness that scared the crap out of the town. If Jasper was on your side, he was practically Santa Claus, but if he was against you, he was Satan incarnate.

Tonight, he was Santa with pleasant green eyes, pale skin

with rosy cheeks, and light red hair he kept short and neat. He appeared to be in his late forties or early fifties with fine lines framing his eyes and etching his forehead. He was of average height and frame, and to most people, he looked like your friendly neighborhood dad.

Except Evan had seen him fight. His speed and agility were unmatched. Evan still wasn't sure how Jasper had become so strong, but he assumed it was connected to the quantity and type of blood he drank. He had a superior supply, and he was stingy.

Evan decided he didn't want to test Jasper that night. He was probably already stressed with complaints from townspeople about their missing loved ones. His best bet was to tell the truth. Well, the truth-ish.

"I went to go find Thalia's friend, right?" Evan looked over to his adopted sister.

She nodded. "Yeah, and clearly, you didn't find her. She was my best friend." She sniffled, wiping at her eyes.

"We'll find her, sweetheart," Jasper stated, getting up and walking to his daughter. He embraced her.

She placed her head on his chest, letting out short cries.

Jasper looked over to Evan with the same cool eyes. "Continue."

Evan cleared his throat. "I stopped one of the attackers from taking someone and got in a fight with them. I almost died, and a woman offered me some blood. She had gotten separated from her friends, so I stayed with her until she was able to connect with them this morning. We stayed in a hotel near the bazaar."

Jasper smiled. "You forgot to contact us and ease our worrying because of a woman?"

Thalia adjusted and looked sideways at Evan with angry eyes. "That was selfish."

"You must have been quite taken with her." Jasper's smile didn't falter, but his eyes grew chilly.

Evan shifted his footing, looking down at his feet. He knew Jasper well enough now to read between the lines. Jasper wasn't happy, and so far, he didn't think Evan's rationale excused his behavior. "She helped me."

Jasper cocked a brow. "She must have been very pretty."

Evan looked up at his adopted father with wide eyes. "She's beautiful."

"Will you see her again?"

"I hope so."

"I've never heard you talk about a woman before. I hope she was worth our worry. Where does she live?"

Evan stiffened slightly. He really didn't want Jasper knowing that she was from a government town. Jasper hated such towns. However, if he lied, Jasper would know. It was as if he could feel a lie radiating in the air. "She lives in a government town," he mumbled reluctantly.

Jasper held him back by his shoulders, his eyes deceptively pleasant. "Is she human?"

"I'm not sure," Evan stuttered, afraid to tell the full truth. A woman who could bring back the dead? He could only imagine Jasper's intrigue, and he wanted to keep them apart.

"With her all night and you don't know? What did her blood taste like?"

Like almonds and chocolate, he wanted to say, but he still wasn't sure how it could be so sweet. He didn't want to raise Jasper's curiosity any more than he had, so he downplayed the truth. "Sweet."

Jasper gave a nod, patting Evan on the shoulder. "Sweet is always more potent. Must have been delicious. What's her name?"

Evan bit his lip. He really didn't want to tell them anything about her. Giving Jasper any knowledge about Jazmine put her in a precarious position if he ever went looking for her. However, he knew he wouldn't be leaving this room without saying anything. Damn it, he could never do what he wanted when it came to Jasper. Was he that scared of him? Yes, yes he was. "Jazmine. Jazmine St. Clair."

Jasper rubbed his chin. "St. Clair, you say?" Jasper went to sit down at his desk again. He began typing on his computer, not saying anything further.

"I can't believe you met some girl who lives in a government town," Thalia asked with distain, flipping her long hair over her shoulder. "And is now the time to be chasing after some woman. There's a crazy group out there attacking any and everybody. It's not safe to go out. She's just a government loser."

Evan glared at her. "She's not a loser. She's smart and kind."

"Father says we have to stay away from the government. They'd invade our town and separate us all if they could. I heard some of those towns are even kicking out the paranormal due to the violent illness going on. They want to kill our kind."

Evan rubbed his temples, holding back annoyance. "Right, but she's not the government. She's her own person."

Thalia crossed her arms and huffed. "You think you're going to see her again, don't you? You'll never get in a government town."

Jasper sat back in his leather chair, his lips turned up in the slightest of smiles. "I can get you in. I have connections all over. My interest is to build power and allies, not enemies. I don't trust the government, but I'd be stupid not to build allies within. You want to go see your new friend? I support it."

"Dad," Thalia cried.

Evan wasn't a fool. Jasper had his nice moments, but they were always calculated kindness. Evan was still waiting for the day Jasper made known why he was so giving to him. He was sure he'd owe the man a large and dangerous favor.

Jasper raised a hand to quiet Thalia, her eyes on Evan.

"Go see her, but let me know if there is anything interesting I should be aware of."

Evan furrowed his brows in disapproval. "You want me to spy?"

Jasper shrugged. "Just share anything you notice."

"Why are you letting me go? Jazmine doesn't seem like someone who knows any government secrets. She's a web and game designer, and she's not very sociable."

"She sounds lame," Thalia grumbled, crossing her arms.

Jasper leaned back in his chair, clasping his hands on his stomach. "That may be. Does she have a sister named Paige?"

Evan looked to the ceiling, recalling his late-night conversation with Jazmine. He recalled her mentioning her sister's name. Paige sounded about right. "Why?"

Jasper smiled. "Paige is engaged to the deputy governor. So, you see, your Jazmine might have more access than you realize. Go for a visit. Get to know her. Maybe even meet her sister and her future brother-in-law. Don't tell them where you're from. I'll get you a government ID. If you learn anything useful, you'll tell me, right?" Jasper leaned forward, resting his forearms on the desk, still in his Santa face.

Evan gulped. He felt sick. He'd wanted to avoid this very thing. Now he wished he'd lied. He was still getting to know her, but he already had an urge to protect her. Even if it was from his own family.

CHAPTER 6

*J*azmine never received unexpected visitors. So, when her phone rang Monday evening, saying she had an outside visitor at the entrance to the community, she was shocked. When the guard who called her said that the visitor was Evan Kitagawa, she was even *more* surprised.

She'd just left Evan's side the morning prior. Now he was there, without so much as an email to let her know he was coming?

Odd.

She met Evan at a hotel that now served as a visitor's center. Getting into a government town was not as easy as just walking in. The whole area was surrounded by an invisible ward that was managed at only two signed entrances. Before entering, a visitor had to get tested for the supernatural illnesses that killed humans and paranormals unless the visitor was already proven immune. If the visitor was a paranormal, he or she was placed under a magic spell that muted all powers for up to forty-eight hours. Power muting could be extended or shortened depending on who sponsored the visitor. Until the guest was fully welcomed into the community, he or she had to have a guide through the entire stay, and so far, the visits were for no more than a week. Although the government wanted more people joining their towns, they were also very mindful of groups against its resurgence, and so they were cautiously flexible.

Jazmine met Evan in his visitor's room, a second-floor hotel room facing the parking lot. When he opened the door, her heart jumped just a tiny bit. He grinned at her like she was the best thing in the world, and those damn dimples were on full display.

Keep your composure, girl. This cute weirdo just showed up in her town without telling her, and she really didn't know him. What was he up to?

He waved her in, and she cautiously followed. She stood near the door, unsure what to do. "What are you doing here?"

Evan gave her a sheepish look and scratched his head, tousling his short wavy hair. "Sorry, I just came. I should have emailed you, but I wanted to surprise you. In retrospect, that's probably weird, right?"

Jazmine raised her chin, eyeing him with suspicion. "Yes. How did you find me?"

"I remember you saying you lived in a government town not far from the bazaar. I just did a process of elimination. This is the closest one. I'm sorry I came back so soon. I just couldn't... you were on my mind." He looked down at his feet, but she caught a faint blush on his cheeks before he looked away.

Well darn, he was being sweet. Had she really made that much of an impression on him? What if he was just trying to sleep with her after learning how vulnerable she was?

She pressed her lips together and leaned back. She was sure he'd told her he was from a vampire town. How'd he get an ID? "I'm surprised they gave you your own room instead of detaining you until you got a sponsor."

"See the truth is—"

She put a finger to his lips and then pointed upwards. Gosh, his lips were soft. *Not the point, Jaz.* No one could expect a visitor's room to not be bugged with a magic listening spell. They just didn't trust strangers, and something inside her wanted to protect him from saying anything that would get him in trouble. "Do you want to come for a visit to my place? I'd just made dinner when I got the call you were here."

His eyes grew large, and he nodded.

"Great, come with me." She waved him on, and they left the hotel in silence.

Evan leaned towards her when they left the building. "Did you not want to talk in there?"

She shook her head. "I have a feeling that whatever you are going to tell me could get you in trouble, and there are people listening in. There are people listening in everywhere, really. If you're not part of this town, you don't get full trust. Even if you're part of another government town." *And especially if you're part of a vampire town.* She didn't say that last part just in case there were other ears.

They got in her tiny, two-seater car and headed to her apartment. Cars only ran with magic nowadays, and the smaller the car, the less magic you had to use. Getting someone to start a car for you was pretty pricy. Even with a two-seater, Jazmine had to pay for the magic start in monthly installments that would take a couple of years. The only cars that were cheap to start were the newly made *magical* cars that had come out from a few manufacturers several months ago. However, Jazmine didn't think she'd ever be able to afford one of those. Plus, she was fine with her thirteen-year-old car. It got her from point A to point B, and she never really went anywhere.

"It's safe to talk in my car and my place. I get them wiped for spells and got wards put on so no one can put spells on my car," she stated.

Evan looked over to her with a raised brow. "Paranoid someone will listen in?"

She shrugged. "I don't trust the government fully. I've read some things on the internet.

Some are just conspiracy theories, but others seem plausible. Pictures of things you wouldn't believe. Killing people who speak out too much. Some towns were in cahoots with whatever group was stealing paranormals to use their blood for that superhuman serum not too long ago."

He nodded slowly. "I heard about that."

"So, how'd you get into town so easily?"

He gave a shaky grin. "I have an ID."

She narrowed her eyes, glancing over to him. "It's a fake?"

He nodded slowly. "Didn't think they'd let in a vampire from a non-government town. Especially after the attacks."

She should report him. It would be the responsible thing to do. But she couldn't deny that she was happy to see him. She maybe didn't really want to see him go. Also, if she reported him, they would arrest him, and he'd never see the light of day. And that could encourage wrath from his home town, and they could attack them just to get Evan back.

He was silly for taking such a risk, but she wouldn't penalize him for it. Of course, she wouldn't be stupid either. She wasn't sure she fully trusted him, so she'd be keeping an eye on him. For all she knew, he was a spy trying to get secrets from her town and thought he had an in with her. He would be sorely disappointed because she knew nothing going on in her town.

"Well, since you have an ID and a sponsor in me, they let you keep your magic, huh?" she asked.

He nodded.

She pulled up to the apartment, and they entered the garage.

He sighed. "I guess I should tell you the whole truth since that's the right thing to do."

She scrunched her nose in disapproval. "You lied about something else?"

He rubbed the back of his neck and gave her a sorrowful look. "I actually don't live in Philly. I live in D.C. I only lied about it so that I could spend more time with you."

Jazmine nodded slowly. She wasn't sure if she was freaked out or happy. The last time a guy had shown any interest in her in real life, because the internet didn't count, was in fourth grade. Someone had put a box of chocolates on her desk, but they hadn't signed the note. To this day, she didn't know who'd given her the candy. For all she knew, it could have actually been her mother. "I guess I should be flattered. Assuming I believe you." She did, but she couldn't make him too comfortable now. She parked the car, and they got out, heading to the elevator.

"And something else."

She rolled her eyes. "Okay, well, hold off until we get to my place. You're unbelievable, do you know that?"

He shoved his hands into his pockets and looked down at the floor. "I try not to be."

She snorted, and they made the rest of the way to her place in silence. Once inside, she led him to the living room, and they sat down. "What you have to say next will depend on whether you get any food."

Evan stared at her with wide eyes, tapping his chest with two fingers. "My heart stopped beating."

She frowned.

He grabbed her hand, putting it against his chest.

She again, tried in vain to ignore his solid build through his clothes, but it was no easy task. But that wasn't why he put her hand there, so it was time to be an adult and focus.

At first, she felt nothing, confusion overtaking her, and then, seconds later, his heart beat. She held her hand there for several more seconds, listening as his heart beat took on a more normal pace. She looked up at him, moving her hand away. "What just happened? Did your heartbeat slow and then start up again?"

Evan sighed. "When I woke up last night, my heartbeat was gone. It only just came back."

"Maybe I can only help you for just a short time period?" She had no idea. She still had no clue how she'd gotten his heart to beat at all or how she was able to touch someone living that wasn't her sister.

Evan suddenly jumped up and pointed to her. "Stay right there. I'll be right back. Don't move, okay?"

She nodded and watched him as he left the apartment. She looked around the living room, thoroughly confused. "What's happening?" she asked herself out loud. What if she was like some human defibrillator? Her hands were like the paddles. Only they were a temporary fix. Now that would be a cool power to have.

Less than five minutes later, Evan returned. looking very perturbed.

"What happened? Did someone try to get you for being out without a guide?" she asked, shaking her head.

He put up a finger and looked at his watch, touching the pulse at his neck. Minutes went by, and she let out a confused sigh.

"I barely left a block from here before my heart stopped beating." Evan looked at her with wild eyes. "Then I come back, and in less than five minutes, my heartbeat starts again. And you didn't even touch me this time. Being in your proximity keeps my heart beating. Wow. That's almost poetic."

She gave a nervous snort then quieted down once she saw his face. There was something in his eyes that gave her pause. Admiration. It gave her a little pang in the pit of her stomach.

He rubbed his hands together in excitement. "Do I get to eat? Since I was an undead vampire, we can't eat food. Maybe with my heart beating again, I can."

"Spaghetti and meatballs work?" She asked, standing up.

Maybe he wasn't that excited about her and more about the food. Well, that was a little letdown.

"Jazmine, peanut butter and jelly works for me, so yeah." His grin widened.

The way he said her name, with that baritone heavy voice that didn't seem to fit his young appearance, made her knees weak. "Have a seat at the dining table. I'll fix everything." *And go cool myself off in the kitchen while I'm at it.*

It took her no time to prepare the food, and she grabbed a bottle of wine to bring to the table. She supposed this would be a celebration if he could actually eat.

"This looks amazing," Evan announced, looking down at his plate. He then quickly dug in and shoved a large fork full of pasta in his mouth.

Jazmine held in a breath. So much for table manners. Not to mention, he was taking chances eating that much in one go. If he still couldn't eat, the food would come right back up, and that would really kill the mood.

He closed his mouth and chewed slowly. The way he worked his mouth and then gulped, it seemed almost lewd. She felt like a voyeur watching something naughty. She adjusted in her seat and looked away until she heard a moan. She quickly looked back at him and saw that his head was lowered. He took another bite and then moaned again. Okay, he was really pushing it. She wondered if she should give him some privacy. When he finally looked up at her, she saw that his eyes were watery.

"I can eat," he said in a soft voice. "I haven't eaten food in six years. You've changed my world. Again. And this is delicious." There was sincerity in his voice, and she was certain he was telling the truth.

Feeling self-conscious under his gaze, she shrugged and picked up her fork to eat. "It's nothing special."

"Can I stay here with you for a while?" he asked, continuing to eat.

She dropped her fork and looked at him with an open mouth in surprise. Well, seeing as she was able to keep his heart going, perhaps she shouldn't be so surprised that he wanted to stick by her side for a while.

"I know it's weird, but the hotel sucks, and I like hanging out with you." He continued to talk as he shoveled food in his mouth too fast to possibly chew. Was he even tasting it anymore?

"Don't you need to go home?"

"No, this is my vacation. Kind of. I want to keep eating and breathing."

"Oh." She felt slightly dejected. He really only wanted to be around her because of what she could do for him, not because he really liked her. It made sense. Maybe she should be happy someone finally *wanted* to be around her.

He put his fork down and grabbed her hand, breaking her thoughts. "Look, I won't mooch off you. I have money. Just for a little while, can I stay? I'll sleep on the couch. I'll clean. I won't bother you. I'll be asleep all day anyway. I do want to get to know you better."

"And continue to eat."

"It definitely is a pull." Evan gave her hand a squeeze and another dimpled grin. "I can make it worth your while. Anything you want?"

She raised an eyebrow. What she wanted was to get rid of her stupid power, but he couldn't help with that. She frowned in thought. Well, there was something he could help with, but she thought it sounded weird even in her head.

She slowly pulled her hand back, not wanting to make things more awkward. "I have a proposal."

Evan leaned into the table, an eager look on his face.

"I'll let you stay for a week if you help me to experience touching." God, that sounded so awful out loud.

However, Evan's face didn't betray any look of disgust. "Deal."

She shook her head quickly. "What? Just like that? Don't you want to know what kind of touching?"

He picked up his fork and began to dig into his food again. "No. Not really. I figure you aren't talking about groping me, not that I'd mind that." He chuckled.

She grimaced in embarrassment back.

"You just want human contact from being so isolated. I can't blame you. People take for granted the power of touch. Even the most innocent of caresses." He grinned at her.

He said he wasn't a flirt, but she was pretty sure that's what he was doing. She pressed her lips together in a satisfied smile. Then a bothersome thought pushed its way into her mind. "Crap, my sister's going to come by and ask questions about why you're here."

"Tell her I'm a friend you met on the internet." He shoveled a large forkful of food in his mouth again.

"That will not make things better." She gave a hollow laugh thinking of her sister's shocked reaction. "But not a bad idea. I can say because you said I could touch you and not die, I had to meet you in person, and we hit it off. I'll tell her you're a zombie, like Theo."

Evan frowned. "Why not tell the truth?"

"Because if she finds that out, she'll want to study you. She'd want to see if there's anything in you that can cure my death touch."

"That's not so bad. I don't mind."

Jazmine cracked up on that one. "You're sweet, but my sister's version of 'studying' you will probably mean dissection."

Evan bowed his head quickly. "Zombie it is."

"And I'll have to get you colored contacts in case you go all scary red-eyed vampire again. That'll be a dead giveaway that you aren't a zombie, no pun intended." She laughed again at her own joke then felt silly when he only grinned at her. She took a sip of her wine, glad to not be drinking alone.

Sometimes, Theo drank with her but he was mostly with Matt these days, so if she wanted a drink, it was solo.

"You have access to contacts?"

She gave a slight raise of her shoulders. "This is a government town. We have access to just about anything as long as it's deemed legal."

Evan grinned like a little boy. She noticed he smiled a lot, and each time, it seemed so genuine. She wondered what it was like to be so light-hearted. Had he ever killed an innocent person? He couldn't have and still be so seemingly carefree.

"So, we're roomies for a while," he stated. "I'm very excited about this, Jazmine."

Even how he said her name made her heart thump. She was not going to fall for him. The very thought terrified her. Love wasn't a real possibility for someone like her.

For now, she was just going to be happy with having a new friend and hope her sister didn't find out about her new roommate.

CHAPTER 7

*A*fter dinner, they talked and played video games until Jazmine fell asleep on the couch, leaving Evan wide awake. He lay on the floor and gazed up at her, resting his head on the large book bag he'd brought with him. She was beautiful, even when she slept. Her full lips parted slightly, and she breathed heavily. Her long lashes fluttered against her smooth skin, and thick strands of hair hung over her face.

He sat up and gently moved the hair behind her ears, relishing in the feel of the softness. What the hell was wrong with him? He was being a creeper, but he couldn't help it. He was beginning to really like this girl. His heart beat faster than normal. Then again, what was normal for an undead vampire brought back to life? Maybe this was the way his heart should beat, and he'd simply forgotten.

He sighed. He was so confused with her. He wanted a simple life, but she had come and shook him up. What was he doing with her? He was really going on instinct.

At first, he'd wanted answers. Then he'd wanted just to enjoy the perks of living, but now he wanted more. More what? She'd given him more than he could have ever hoped.

And what did she want in return? To just hold hands? It didn't seem like a fair trade. Was he taking advantage of her? She seemed like a smart woman. She understood her deal. He actually felt sad when he thought about it.

He'd gone two years alone without human touch, but he'd still petted animals. And now he had access to human connection, not that he ever actively desired it, and he was taking it for granted. The loneliness she must feel being isolated for most of her life in an apartment was palpable. Had anyone cared for her when she was hurt? Hugged her when she was sad? Was it just her sister and Theo?

A frown etched its way on her face.

Was she having a nightmare? Was she uncomfortable on the couch? He wondered if he picked her up and put her on her bed if she'd wake up. He didn't want to disturb her, but he also didn't want to leave her on the couch.

He decided to chance it and lifted her in his arms.

She murmured something unintelligible and rested her head on his shoulder.

He caught a whiff of her scent, like coconut and vanilla. Sweet, just like the taste of her blood. His mouth watered, and his fangs dropped in spite of himself.

Damn it. He was being a perve again. This girl was too sweet to be around him. He really had to watch himself. He tried to retract his fangs, but they were being stubborn. He placed her on the bed and pulled the covers over her. When he moved to leave, she grabbed his hand. He covered his exposed fangs with his other hand, not wanting to scare her with his appearance even though her eyes were still closed.

"Don't go," she whispered.

"Okay," he replied, bending down to get on the floor, but she moved backwards and lifted the covers.

He froze, looking at the patterned blue bedspread. They'd been drinking, and he knew she was slightly tipsy but not drunk. Did she know what she was asking? Maybe she was really sleeping, and this was all some sort of sleep-walking type thing. He didn't want her waking up in the morning and screaming because a stranger was beside her. Then again, maybe this was part of the whole touching deal.

She opened one eye and looked up at him. "I know you're a vampire, and you don't really sleep at night but just lay by me for a little bit. I've read that body heat can be nice, and I just want to know what that feels like. Unless it's too awkward," she said. "I have to work in the morning so please make up your mind. My arm is getting tired holding these covers up."

Evan straightened up and slid into bed beside her. He lay on his back, stiff, his reawakened heart beating fast in his chest.

"In the movies, they do something called spooning. You get on your side, and I move up in front of you," Jazmine stated. "Do you know how to do it?"

Of course, he did. He'd even done it a few times, but now didn't seem like the appropriate time to tell her that. It was actually better that she wanted to spoon. That way, she didn't see his blood need.

"And put your fangs away, they're unsettling."

He closed his eyes in embarrassment as he turned on his side. This time he was successful with putting his cravings away.

"Okay. You ready?" she asked.

"Uh, yeah."

She moved toward him, and he thought of all unexciting things to ignore the fact that her bottom was touching his groin. If she moved back any closer, things would really get awkward.

She thrummed the bed with her fingers. "Aren't you supposed to do something with your free arm?"

"Yes," he replied, before putting his arm over her waist. "Are you comfortable?"

"Yes. You?"

"Uh-huh." His voice just cracked. Why did his voice have to do that? He was a nerd. He *thought* he was cool, but no, he was really a thirteen-year-old boy inside a twenty-one-year-old man.

"This is nice. You're so warm." She let out a sigh. "I shouldn't have done this. I think I might miss it when you leave."

"Well, then I won't leave," he joked. But was he joking? He wasn't looking forward to returning home.

He had no plans to spy on Jazmine's town or take advantage of her kindness. Jasper had given Evan a week to be there. Evan had no idea what he was going to tell Jasper when he returned. He needed to think of a plan because Jasper would not be satisfied that there was nothing of interest to share. He'd have to make something up. But that was for later.

For now, he had to focus on not rising to attention as Jazmine insisted on snuggly closer to him and almost purring like a kitten. Didn't she know what kind of effect she had on him? Maybe not. If she'd never touched anyone for ten years, it stood to reason she'd never had a boyfriend or a date of any sort. Therefore, she'd probably never laid next to a guy, let alone had sex.

He was her first bed partner. He took a bit of joy in that. Innocence rolled off her in waves, and he found that confusingly exciting. She was the type of woman who would want a relationship. He was not boyfriend material. He was a grumpy loner whose romance game was zero and none.

She snuggled closer to him and then froze.

He froze too. Damn it. His body had betrayed him. He was as hard as a rock right now. His heart sank to his stomach in panic. Maybe she really didn't feel anything. Did she even know the male anatomy that well? Maybe she thought it was his leg? No, she couldn't be *that* clueless. She had probably not had sex ed before the world changed, but she had to have seen old magazines or videos on the internet by now? Hadn't she? And if she had, then she would surely know she'd brought him to life. Had she done that on purpose?

She cleared her throat and moved forward a bit but said nothing.

He was sweating. This was not sexy. He should just roll off the side of the bed and crawl under it until the next evening. He couldn't even pretend he was asleep because as a vampire, this was basically his late morning, early afternoon.

What should he do? Should he say something? That would be weird, right? And what the hell would he even say?

No. He should just play it as normal. It was her own fault for basically grinding on him.

What? She probably didn't know any better, and he could have moved back.

"You're pretty well endowed. If I had known that, I would not have gotten so close. I apologize," she said, with no tone of embarrassment at all.

His heart stopped but not for real this time. Should he be embarrassed, flattered? He was both. And the way she said it, as if just saying 'nice shoes.' Like it was nothing. Yeah, it really had been too long since she'd been around people. Hadn't her sister or Theo talked to her about things you shouldn't and should say out loud?

Then again, why should she change? Her honesty and directness were refreshing. He would always know where he stood with her. There would be no mind games. He should take some comfort in that.

"No problem. I should have had better control," he replied in a cracked voice. Damn it, his inner eighth grader just showed back up. Okay, so he couldn't be as cool as her about it.

This woman amazed him more and more. He had never

been so intrigued by anyone. When he'd first joined his town, it had been overwhelming and exciting, but as the years rolled on, he found most vampires mundane. The arrogance, the overt sex appeal, the elitism. They were either too cool or too emo for anything. There were few awkward or silly vampires in his community.

Jazmine was neither cool nor emo. She was awkward, kind, and smart. She was unique, and he was falling for it all. This only made him want to beat his head against a wall because he knew it wouldn't last. He couldn't stay here. She was too precious and deserved better. He was just going to end up hurting her even if he didn't mean to.

~

*J*azmine spent the next day working diligently and *not* trying to think about the super-hot guy sleeping in her bed. She still had to make a living, and distractions were never her thing. When she'd finally finished for the day, she crept to her room to check in on Evan and grab some clothes. Honestly, she'd "checked in" on him several times that day. She couldn't help it. Him being there still felt surreal.

When she walked in, Evan was already awake but still lying on the bed.

She grinned, happier than she wanted to admit at his presence. "Evening. Don't mind me. Just grabbing some clothes. If you're hungry, there's some food in the fridge. I don't have access to blood, but I'll see if Theo can help." She opened her closet door and looked through it for an appropriate outfit for the night.

"Going somewhere?" Evan asked, still on the bed.

"There's a town hall meeting at seven about the attacks. I usually don't go to those type of things, but being that I was *there*, I was requested." She grabbed a long-sleeved pinstriped blouse and a pair of jeans. "I can stand at the back away from people. I have a hazmat suit I wear as well."

Evan sat up and rubbed his eyes. "You wear a full hazmat suit?"

She furrowed her brows together and slowly tapped her chin. "I typically do, but you know, I could get those temporary warding tattoos put back on. They worked well at the bazaar until I rubbed them off."

"They come off that easily? That's risky."

She shook her head, looking at him. "They come off with a special solution I carried. But they do eventually wear off after a week."

"If no one can touch you, how'd the artist put them on you?" He stood up and stretched.

She tried to ignore the bit of well-toned stomach peaking from the bottom of his shirt. Lying next to him until she'd fallen asleep had been...comforting. He'd stayed with her for a while before she felt him eventually get up and head to the living room. When she got up that morning, she'd learned he'd spent the night and early morning reading books, streaming shows and movies, and eating. He'd even baked cookies.

"Magic. Magic is always the answer," she explained. "She just hovered her hands over mine, and these etchings appeared. I think I have time to get to her before the meeting, so stay here. I've got to get Theo to go with me."

He shook his head. "I go where you go."

She paused before heading to her bathroom. "Why?"

"I came here for you. I want to be by your side for the time we're both awake."

"Speaking of awake. I'm surprised you're up so early. It's only five. Since it's the summer, that's kind of early for you, no?" She twisted her lips in thought. "It might be because your heart is beating now?" She chuckled to herself as she finished thinking that through. Nothing was funny, but it was interesting watching someone *actually* come to life.

~

They went to the tattoo artist's shop and were able to get squeezed in. When they were done, they drove to the town meeting hall, which was located in the local high school auditorium.

"Is this the whole town?" Evan asked as they parked the car in a packed parking lot. They'd gotten there early but had just lucked out at getting the last available parking space in the lot.

Jazmine shook her head.

She had the helmet of her hazmat suit off, but she still insisted on wearing the suit. She had the tattoos, but it seemed her paranoia and fear of upsetting others by not having it on was strong. She said it was for her own comfort as much as others, but Evan hoped she didn't plan to put the helmet on. He could imagine it was stifling.

"Oh no," she said. "It couldn't fit the whole town or even just the adults, so it's first come first serve as far as spacing. There are overflow rooms, and the meeting is being streamed for people to watch and raise questions. We've got like ten thousand people in our town."

Evan leaned back, impressed. "Wow, that's a lot."

Jazmine opened her car door and pursed her lips. "Our town used to be a combination of an area called Crystal City and Pentagon City. It had about forty-five thousand residents combined in the Pre-World. Then the supernatural sickness killed half the population, as you know, but there were even fewer survivors when you consider the supernatural killing people, people just killing each other for whatever reasons, and people fleeing the area for safer places. As if any place is totally safe even with wards." She juggled her keys in her hand as she continued spouting out facts.

That was so cute.

"There was also a lot of destruction, making it mostly inhabitable for a while. And the effort to kill and push out the man-eating plant life and monsters was tremendous. They had to rebuild and restart. Then, of course, they had to get people to want to come back to the area after it was so devastated. So, in the end, an area that once had forty-five thousand people and now having only twenty percent of its former population isn't really large. However, compared to other government towns, we range in the mid to large category. We got more people because there are less government towns in Virginia."

He raised his eyebrows, trying to decide if he was impressed with the history lesson or the fact that she kept going.

She got out of the car, grabbing her helmet.

He followed, deciding to be impressed. "Wow, you ran through that like a human encyclopedia. How do you know all that?"

She looked at him as if he'd just asked her for the answer to one plus one. "I live in isolation and spend most of my time on the internet and reading books. I find it fascinating to learn about areas during the Pre-World as compared to what they are now. People keep saying that fifty percent of the world population died when the paranormal came, but we all know it's more than that. We haven't counted those who were killed in fighting battles or big monsters or even from regular illnesses because they couldn't get medical access in time or because they didn't have access to electricity or medication that stopped being produced when this all began. Or even those who died from other paranormals, whether on purpose or not."

She looked away, and her voice quieted down when she

said the last part. He tried to see her face, but she was turned too far away. The way her voice trailed off at the last part, he wondered if she had hurt someone. It was certainly possible. How else would she have figured out that her touch was deadly?

He could only imagine learning that horror. How young had she been? How many people had she touched before she'd learned it was more than a coincidence? He felt over-whelmingly sorry for her just then. He wanted to grab her and hold her tight, but he wasn't sure she'd appreciate that. There was a hardness to her he was still learning about. She wanted touch, but it felt more like an experience to him. Like she wanted to hold hands or spoon to learn about it, not because she particularly liked him or desired that human connection.

Maybe he could change that.

CHAPTER 8

"*N*ormally, I avoid going to town hall meetings," Jazmine explained as they headed inside the high school. "I wish my sister didn't make me come."

She decided to shift subjects because she didn't want Evan going too far into questioning her last statement. She was sure he could put two and two together and realize that for her to have a death touch, she would have had to kill people to learn about her magic. Most people made that easy leap once she explained her magic, and that made her even more of a social pariah. While her sister got to be the merciful healer, she was the bringer of death who could apparently only befriend undead beings. Not even dogs and cats could come around her.

She let out a deep breath and shook, getting rid of her pity party table for one.

Evan gave her side-eye. "Does your sister always boss you around?"

Jazmine nodded. "She's basically my mother, and I don't want to alienate her. She protects me. She's sacrificed a lot for me. There were places that didn't want me around but wanted her. Places that were very comfortable for a teenager to be. But she never left me. She fought for me to get a chance here. They wanted to lock me up until I was an adult. She fought to keep me free. I don't want to ever do anything to take advantage of her and all that she's done. Especially now that she's in the lime light. Nor do I want to be the obstacle holding back her fiancé's future plans. He might want to run for president one day."

Evan patted her shoulder. "You're a good person. He should be lucky to have you in his family."

Jazmine snorted but didn't say anything. Evan didn't need to know that her soon-to-be brother-in-law looked at her like some weirdo freak he wished would disappear. He wasn't here to listen to her life's sob stories. That would only run him away, and for now, she liked him with her.

When they got into the auditorium, the place was already packed despite it still being early. They stayed in the back, away from the doors and others. She attempted to put on her helmet, and Evan grabbed it from her with a grimace on his face.

"That's overkill. You have the tats and the suit already," he said. "It's hot enough in here. No need in passing out as well."

Jazmine stood rigid, ready to jump at any moment if anyone came too close. It didn't matter to her if she had the tattoos on or a hazmat suit, she was forever going to be on edge around most people, even with Evan. Some habits were hard to break.

The night before, when he'd spooned her, she'd thought she would actually melt. It'd been intimate, exciting, and comfortable all at the same time. Now, she understood why so many people did it in the old movies and TV shows she watched. It was the best thing ever. All she could think about was doing it again.

Her thoughts were interrupted when a woman walked onto the small stage. "Good evening, everyone," she said. There were a few chairs around the podium where some of the officials sat. "We are ready to begin the meeting. Please take your seats and quiet down."

An arm brushed against Jazmine, and she jumped into Evan on her other side. She looked up in alarm at Theo and Matt.

"Relax, lady," Theo said with a smile. He looked past her at Evan with narrowed eyes. "Is this stranger danger?"

"Evan Kitagawa." Evan outstretched a hand, and Theo shook it.

They both stared at each other silently for a moment, as if sizing each other up. Evan placed a protective hand on Jazmine's back as he held Theo's gaze.

Theo looked at Evan with a raised eyebrow before finally speaking. "I'm Theo, and this is my boyfriend, Matt."

Matt, a tall, lanky blond, gave a lazy smile and head nod.

Evan grinned with what looked like relief to Jazmine. "Nice to meet you both."

An older woman turned and shh'd them. Upon seeing Jazmine, her eyes grew large, and she whispered to another woman beside her.

The other woman looked back at Jazmine and frowned. "You really shouldn't be here," she spat before pushing her friend out of the row and further away from them.

Jazmine tried to shrink herself, feeling as if she was taking up too much space now. She noticed from her right, a family scurrying away as well, and suddenly, it seemed as if the space around them grew larger.

"Ugh, death girl is here," whispered some teens as they scurried through the entrance.

Death girl. That was the name she'd been given when she'd first arrived and people had found out about her. They hadn't seen her kill. Just the idea made her a mark. Although without gloves, there were a few eyewitnesses to her killing plant-life and fruits and vegetables growing outside.

Something flew from her left, and Evan reached out his

hand inches from her face, grabbing it. He opened it, and they could see it was a large chunk of ice.

Had someone thrown ice at her? It wasn't the first time people in this town had thrown things at her. She'd once had a dead bird chucked at her. For a while, anything that had died without clear cause had been blamed on her. In the first year of her arrival, she'd been monitored constantly, even in her apartment, through cameras and looking spells. They'd wanted to ensure she didn't leave unattended to kill. Her only privacy had been in the bathroom, and she was never fully certain of that.

"We should go," she whispered, practically shaking now with anger and unease.

"Screw 'em," Theo said loudly and grabbed Jazmine's hand. "You're covered and at a safe distance. You aren't the one out here killing people."

Evan grabbed her other hand but didn't look at her.

She knew what they were doing, and it helped more than they could have realized.

They focused back on the stage, and she tried to concentrate as the governor talked about the attacks and gave her condolences to those who were missing. She stated that the deputy would lead the investigation into finding the kidnapped and the attackers, then gave him the microphone to summarize their efforts and plans.

Bryant Montgomery, the deputy governor, and Paige's fiancé, looked like what you would expect of a Pre-World young congressman. He was of average height and build, with cropped curly dark brown hair, and light brown eyes. There was nothing extraordinarily unique about him beyond his powers as a telekinetic. Jazmine found him as dull as cardboard. Every show of emotion seemed strategic, and he never appeared authentic to her. She really couldn't understand what Paige saw in him beyond some probable idea of security that he could give as a government leader. Jazmine tried to understand that. As someone who was always protecting others, she could see how Paige would value being with someone who could finally protect her.

"As Governor Jackson said, these attacks are not the first. However, this latest one was the largest. We've been paying close attention. The common themes are that they happen at night, they only take paranormals, and they have the ability to teleport. The attacks usually occur outside of towns, so it's possible they don't have the ability to break wards. We don't know where this group is taking them or what they do with them. If you must travel, travel during the day time and not by foot."

Jazmine snuck a look at Evan. They'd been lucky they hadn't been snatched when they'd made that walk to the hotel the other night, but since it had occurred right after the raid, that might explain why they hadn't run into trouble.

"We also believe these attackers to be vampires. We've gotten reports from those that attended the bazaar this past weekend of seeing red eyes and fangs from those who were grabbing patrons. These are signs of vampires. I'll take questions now."

Jazmine wondered why she'd *had* to come if this was all the briefing. She could have stayed home for this.

There were already lines forming at the microphone stands throughout the space. An older man spoke first. "Could these attacks be related to that new paranormal illness going around? If the vampires had red eyes, then they were in bloodlust. Usually, that means the vampires aren't in control anymore. They could be snatching folks and drinking them dry."

Gasps and cries could be heard in the audience.

People needed hope. No one wanted to think that their loved one was actually dead.

Bryant held up a hand to quiet the crowd. "I just want to make it clear that vampires who are not in bloodlust *can* get red eyes, usually when fighting or overdrinking or of thirst. It does not mean they have gone feral. From what we know of the paranormal illness, it is drug related and has a side effect of causing regression. While in the regressive state, with the magic-based drugs in his or her system, that being can infect another. Also, when in a regressive state, a being does not have their full mental faculties. *These* attacks are very different. The attackers move with purpose, and they work together. Had this been one person doing the kidnapping, we would be more open to the possibility that this was a regressive attack. However, several accounts let us know that these kidnappers worked together. They had a plan and were organized. They only took paranormals and not non-magic humans."

"I don't understand," stated a woman at the other microphone stand. "Vampires are fast, but they don't teleport, right?"

Jazmine looked over to Evan again. Good question. She'd forgotten all about that.

Seemingly feeling her eyes on him, he turned to her. "We don't," he whispered. "I had the same question."

Bryant nodded. "We thought about that as well. It's our belief that they have been enhanced. It's very possible that they got the help from a witch or warlock who gave them the ability to transport quickly. This is a dark group that we cannot underestimate. We must be vigilant."

"Any idea where they could be located?" another townsperson asked.

"We don't know for certain. However, the attacks, as they've been reported, are only happening in this state, the district, and Maryland. It's very possible this group is in the area, so keep your eyes open and your guard up. Patrol will be heightened now, and we are working with our allied towns to share information."

"What about that vampire town nearby? The one in

D.C.?" asked another man. "Has anyone asked if they're behind it? I wouldn't be surprised. A town full of just vampires can't be too friendly to others. They probably look at the rest of us like food."

The crowd started to murmur in agreement with some people suggesting that they attack the town.

Bryant tapped the mic for attention. "We've considered that. We've requested a visit but were denied. We are now awaiting a response to at least have a meeting at a neutral location to discuss the issue."

Jazmin looked up at Evan out of the corner of her eye. Where had he said he was from?

He stiffened slightly as Bryant continued talking.

"They're a very closed off town, so we don't know what goes on there. If we attempt to force our way in, that could start a battle, and we must be very careful about taking that step. Especially if they aren't behind this. That may change later, but for now, we prefer this way in case they have anything to share with us."

Theo elbowed her and tilted his head towards the door, and the four of them exited.

"I had to get out of there," he stated as they left the building. "They don't know anything more than we know."

Jazmine tapped Evan, and they turned to leave as well.

"Where are you staying?" Theo asked, looking to her temporary house guest.

Evan tilted his head and raised his eyebrows, looking as innocent as possible for a grown man. "With Jazmine."

Theo frowned, crossing his arms. "Shouldn't you be in guest housing? How long are you going to be here? Why are you even here? Where are you from?"

Jazmine sighed. She knew Theo was only looking out for her, but he was sounding more like a cop than a friend. "He's visiting me from another government town in Philadelphia."

Theo tilted his head and narrowed his eyes in suspicion. "Why?"

Matt touched Theo's arm and gave him a look, one that said, drop it. "Can't our baby girl have a new friend?" he asked in a soft voice. He looked over to Evan with a knowing smile. "Be good to our Jaz. Give her all the hugs I can't."

"How about we not," Theo grumbled, glaring at Evan. "With all that's going on, the last thing we need are strangers coming around. Jazmine is very innocent. She doesn't need anyone taking advantage of her."

Jazmine sighed loudly. "Please stop talking about me like I'm some little kid, new to the world."

Evan reached for her hand and squeezed it.

She looked down at their clasped hands in shock. She still wasn't use to the contact. It felt dream-like.

"I like Jaz," Evan began. "I have no intentions of using her. I've never met anyone as amazing as her." He looked to Jazmine with a bright smile, and she was sure she was blushing. Hopefully, her coloring was too deep to show it.

"We know she's amazing. You don't have to tell us," Theo grumbled, although the look in his eyes softened. He pointed a finger in Evan's chest. "If you do anything at all to hurt her, I will eat your brains. Literally."

"Please don't," Jazmine said, pulling Evan with her. "We need to go before my sister comes. Don't let her know Evan is staying with me. Bye."

"Our little baby's growing up," Matt said in a pretend crying voice, dabbing invisible tears from the corners of his eyes.

"Keep your legs crossed," Theo shouted behind them.

Jazmine rolled her eyes. "Please ignore them. I can't recall the last time I was embarrassed so this is a special occasion. Come on, let's walk faster. I really don't want to see my sister."

"And why is that?" came a shrill voice behind them.

CHAPTER 9

*P*aige stood in the front of the door leading to the parking lot, hands on her hips and eyes narrowed at Evan.

"What are you doing out?" Jazmine asked, more than annoyed. "Isn't the meeting still going on?"

"Yes. I asked you to stay for the *whole* meeting. Who's this?" Paige questioned, looking to Evan and then their joined hands.

Jazmine let go of him. "He's a friend I met in an online group."

Evan stepped forward and offered his hand to Paige. "You must be Jazmine's sister. I'm Evan. Nice to meet you."

Paige shook his hand, looking at Jazmine with a questioning glance before looking back to him. "You touched my sister. Even when she's wearing those special tattoos and the suit, people still won't come close. What are you?"

Jazmine's eyes grew wide. *Stick to the plan, Evan,* she said in her mind, wishing she had telepathy. Luckily, she was able to secure contacts that day, and Evan had them on so his eyes wouldn't go red by mistake. As long as he kept his fangs from shooting out, things would be fine.

"I'm a zombie. A non-reanimated one like Theo," he replied with a careful smile.

Paige assessed him as if weighing his words for the truth. "Huh," was all she said in response. "You aren't from town. Where do you come from?"

As long as Evan was in a government database, they would be okay. Jazmine hoped the fake ID was more than just a picture and that he was in the system because Paige, or someone she hired, would be looking.

"Philadelphia," Evan replied with confidence.

She really hoped he was smart enough to know Paige would check.

"What's your last name?"

"Kitagawa."

"Huh," she said again. "And you came here to..."

"Visit your sister. I really like her. I'd like to seriously date her. She's very special to me."

Jazmine stared at him with large eyes. *Don't go too far*, she thought. He was talking as if he planned to stick around.

Paige's eyes were unreadable. "Interesting."

Jazmine cocked her head toward her sister. Interesting? What did that mean? Did Paige think no one could really like her?

Paige rudely shooed Evan away. "Well, I need to talk to my sister for a bit, so can you hang out with her later?"

"No, he can't," Jazmine began. "Look, he's staying with me." She braced herself for the lecture.

Paige opened her mouth and looked over to Evan then back at Jazmine. "That doesn't sound like the smartest thing to do."

Evan gave a wide grin. "I'm harmless."

Paige rolled her eyes. "Of course, you are." She looked to her sister with angry eyes. "Jazmine, a word." Paige didn't wait for a response and grabbed Jazmine by the arm, leading her away and leaving Evan to stand alone in the parking lot.

"I know, I know," Jazmine began. "It's crazy, but he's fine. He's a good guy. Really."

"We can talk about your stupid life choices another time. Put that man in a hotel tonight," Paige replied, pointing in Evan's direction.

"I'm not a child."

"Then don't make stupid decisions. Anyway." She waved a hand in front of her face. "You've been requested to do something for your town."

Jazmine squinted her eyes. "Come again?"

"The reason I wanted you to come tonight is because the governor is putting together a team to find these paranormal attackers. They're going to place people in locations they believe will be attacked next. Prime areas. We know the attackers haven't hit the same place twice. Your name came up."

Jazmine crossed her arms, curious. "In what way?"

Paige looked away, frowning. "They want to set up a sort of sting operation. I don't know the lingo. They think if someone tried to grab you, you could take them out when you touch them. So, don't wear those temporary tattoos when you go."

They wanted her to be bait. Nice. She had absolutely no experience in this kind of thing. She could have been captured herself at the bazaar, and now they— no, her sister was telling her to risk her life? "Do you *want* me to go?"

Paige looked back at her with incredulous eyes. "Are you kidding me? Of course not. You're my little sister. I would never want you to put yourself in danger. I've protected you all this time. Why would I stop caring now?"

Jazmine shrugged. "Because your husband-to-be told you to."

Paige sighed and placed her hands on Jazmine's shoulder. "Just because I'm getting married doesn't mean I don't care about you anymore. And Bryant likes you."

Jazmine made a pfft sound and shook her head. "This was probably all his idea."

"He's a logical thinker, just like you."

Jazmine groaned. "Please don't compare me to him. What if I don't want to do this? Are they making me?"

Paige moved her hands away, and they hung at her sides helplessly. "You shouldn't say no," she said in a low voice, her words clip.

"Why?"

"Because it's your civic duty," said a male voice behind her. "Your contribution to the community."

She turned and faced Bryant, who approached them, a man dressed in all black behind him. Most likely, his bodyguard, Jazmine surmised.

Bryant stopped about six feet away from her, giving her a nod. "You have a special gift, Jazmine. Let's finally put it to good use."

"I see." She put her hands on her hips and twisted her lips. "So, what do you want me to do? Go walking up and down dark alleyways at midnight alone? Then when some creeper tries to grab me, I get them back. And we can only hope whatever grabs me is part of this group because, as the old song my grandparents use to play goes, the freaks come out at night. I could be eaten by a giant monster instead of getting captured."

Bryant gave her a thin smile that failed to reach his eyes. "We wouldn't send you just anywhere. The goal is to not get you hurt. If you can get an attacker to grab you, they will die. Then we can get a necromancer to bring them back and interrogate them. We can also study the body to determine how they can teleport. It's a solid plan, don't you think?"

Yeah, except for her being bait part. She had to admit it wasn't a horrible plan. However, the thought of her being out, possibly among other people without her tattoos, scared her. What if someone mistakenly touched her? Was this trap worth it?

"Do I have a choice?"

Bryant threw his hands out to the side and lowered his lids, his fake smile becoming lazy. "We all have a choice. Yours is to do this and have your community be forever grateful or to not do it and face any...consequences."

She didn't like how he said that. What did it mean? Punishment? Would she be imprisoned if she refused? She looked over to her sister, who avoided her eyes, wringing her hands in front of her. That didn't seem like Paige. Was she... scared or nervous for Jazmine? This really meant she had no choice here. She had to agree to this. Hadn't she already given back by becoming a hard-working citizen who caused no trouble? She guessed not. This country wasn't a stranger to forcing its citizens to fight on their behalf, why change that now.

She looked back to Bryant. "Fine. Where do you need me to be, and when?"

～

*E*van looked out of the passenger side window as they drove back to Jazmine's place. It wasn't that dark outside this time of year, but the sun was hidden now, and even the brightness in the sky didn't affect him. However, it wasn't the daylight that was currently worrying him. "I'm going with you," Evan stated after Jazmine explained her reluctant mission.

She turned down a quiet street lined with apartments on one side and a park on the other. "That would draw too much attention to you, Evan. I have to do this alone. Although apparently, they will have undercover police around me."

"I don't want to risk it. I'll come with you." He nodded his head, cementing his decision.

A slight smile crossed her lips. "Are you going to go everywhere I go?"

"Yes."

She glanced at him sideways with curious eyes. "Why?"

He turned to her. "Because I want you safe. I can't help it." He really couldn't. He was like a man possessed with the need to protect her. It was almost consuming. He hadn't been this motivated in...ever. It wasn't that he thought she was weak. It was something more. Who was he kidding? It was a lot more. He was crushing on this girl. Not good.

When they got back to the apartment, Jazmine prepared them dinner. It was just leftovers from the previous night, but he enjoyed it just as much, making what Jazmine deemed inappropriate moans of delight as he ate her food.

"You sound like you just had an orgasm," Jazmine muttered in a slightly disapproving tone.

"I think I did," Evan sighed, leaning back in his dining room chair.

He could have sworn the color on her cheeks turned a slight reddish-brown. Had he made her blush? He adjusted in his seat, annoyed that just that thought excited him. *Think different thoughts, Evan, or she'll kick you out for being a perve.*

"So, tell me more about this mission."

She took a sip of wine and rolled her eyes. "I have to go to a club this Saturday. It's in D.C. actually, called Seduction. What a lame and obvious name."

He silently bared his teeth in disapproval. "I know that place. It's, uhm, different." No, he definitely didn't want her going there. She was way too sheltered to stand going to such an establishment. She'd look like bait walking through the door.

Jazmine cut into her pasta as if she were cutting steak but then paused upon his response, a look of concern on her face. "How different?"

Evan noted her quirky eating habit as yet another random thing about her he found adorable.

"Evan?" Jazmine looked up at him with large eyes. "You okay?"

He nodded quickly. "Sorry. *Seduction* is not just any type of club. It's an exchange club."

Jazmine frowned, and then her eyes widened again. "Oh, I've read about those. It's a place where vampires and blood donors go. Oh, and also incubi and succubae. It's kind of like a sex club." She said the last part in a whisper.

Evan nodded.

She put a hand to her mouth. "Well, they didn't tell me all that. I'm gonna get made as soon as I walk in the door. I don't have any sexy clothes, and I'm not getting into a compromising situation with anyone. I'm definitely not letting anyone bite me. You were my first and my last." She gave a curt nod and took a bite of her pasta.

Evan chuckled lightly. "I'm honored, which is why I need to go with you. I can't have anyone trying to bite you or take your energy. You're mine."

She stopped chewing and looked at him with unreadable eyes.

Evan instantly reddened and died a little inside. Why had he said that? Seriously, what was wrong with him? He had to play it off. "Mine to protect. I mean, you're mine to protect. Of course, you're your own woman. Not some property. I just feel like I need to watch your back. I am very crappy with words." He lowered his head and wished his hair was slightly longer to cover his eyes.

Jazmine began to chew again. "You're very odd, Evan. Do you know that? Of course, people say that about me, so I really have no room to talk. But I will accept your protection. Bryant will have to just accept that you will be with me."

He smiled, relieved that she seemed to be fine with his recovery answer. Or at the very least, pretended to be.

She pointed slightly to his almost empty plate with her fork. "Are you done eating? I'd like to cuddle on the couch and watch a movie together. If that's okay."

If that was okay? Didn't she know by now that he was totally infatuated with her? He was like a love-sick puppy. If she wanted to cuddle, he'd stop eating right now and do just that. Just the idea of being close to her again excited him.

He nodded eagerly. He really needed to relax. He was embarrassing himself.

They spent the rest of the evening huddled together on the couch with him willing himself to behave.

When the movie ended, Jazmine jumped up and yawned. "I need to go to bed. You don't have to come with me if you aren't tired."

Evan furrowed his brows in confusion. "Actually, I *am* tired."

Jazmine rubbed her eyes. "Looks like your heart beat is really affecting you."

Evan got to his feet as well. "So, when you say 'come with me,' you're inviting me to bed, right?"

Jazmine waved him over to her. "Yes."

Evan shoved his hands in his pockets and rocked back and forth on his heels, containing his excitement. "So, you want me to sleep with you every night?"

Jazmine twisted her lips and wrung her fingers together. "Only if you want to. I can understand if you want your space."

"Well, no, that was the deal. That you get to touch more while I'm here." He touched his chest. "And I am *more* than willing to accommodate. Would you like to lay your head on my chest tonight?"

Jazmine's eyes brightened up. "Yes, I would like that very much."

Evan gave a little grin and grabbed her hand, heading to

the bedroom. He still didn't understand how he'd lucked out on such an arrangement, but he was really enjoying it.

They changed into their sleepwear and positioned themselves on the bed. Jazmine carefully laid her head on his chest, but he could feel that she was tense. "Relax," he whispered in a low voice, wrapping her arm around him.

That only seemed to make her stiffen more. This was only their third night sleeping in a room together, their second in the same bed. When he considered she'd been alone most of her life, he had to be patient and realize this wouldn't come easily.

He rubbed a hand up and down her arm. "Do you mind me asking how you found out about your magic?"

"When I was at the pizza shop with my dad," she answered in a tiny voice. "He was the first person I killed with my touch."

Evan froze momentarily but quickly recovered and continued to stroke her arm. He couldn't imagine having killed a parent, especially at her young age. Why had he asked such a stupid question?

"It was by accident," she continued in a rush. "He grabbed me to get away from the commotion, and he died. Then another woman grabbed me, and she died too. I also killed plants and animals. I hated myself for so long after that. I wanted to die. After my parent's died, my sister and I stayed with an aunt and cousin for a while. My aunt was my dad's sister, and Paige said it was a good idea to not tell them how dad died. She didn't want us getting kicked out. Heck, even my sister looked at me differently when I told her."

He wanted to kiss her head and let her know everything was okay now, but they hadn't crossed that boundary yet, and he didn't want to freak her out. He knew he had to move slowly with her, but the urge to pull her closer was hard to resist. "You think they really would have kicked you out?"

She nodded against his chest. "My aunt was not the nicest

person to begin with. It was hard staying with her and her bratty son. They treated us like burdens, made us do all the undesirable work. And when they learned that my touch could kill, they made me stay in the garage, and whenever I went into the house to use the bathroom, Paige had to clean it from top to bottom. So, of course, I tried not to go often because I didn't want to be a burden to my sister. I would go outside or in a bucket. I'd take showers only a couple of times a week. It was cold, lonely, and scary. I hated it."

Screw it. He kissed the top of her head and soon felt a slight dampness on his chest.

Jazmine lifted her head slightly. "I'm sorry," she said in a tear-clogged voice, wiping at her face.

He gently moved her head back down on his chest. "It's fine."

"Did you kiss my head?"

He nodded. "Yeah. I'm sorry. I should have asked."

"It's okay. My dad used to do that. Thank you. But please don't feel sorry for me. I know we've all been through things here."

"True, but kissing you would never be out of pity for me." In truth, she'd just given him an excuse.

Jazmine gave a nervous cough. "So, eventually, my aunt and cousin passed from the Sickness. After they died, I got a bit of freedom back, but it was still hard. At that time, I was barely twelve, and Paige was only seventeen. I totally depended on her because I couldn't be around people. We were able to barter and get accepted into communities because of her healing abilities. Staying on our own wasn't safe. Then we found this place. But enough about me. How'd you find your town?"

Evan let out a deep breath. He didn't know if this was the best time to say that the town leader had adopted him, but if she had opened up to say her soon to be brother-in-law was a leader, how unfair would it be for him to keep his connection secret? Sure, it wouldn't be what Jasper would want, but he really wasn't here for him. He was here for Jazmine. "Sooo, the head of my town adopted me."

Jazmine shifted and looked up at him with raised brows. "The head of the nearby vampire town is your dad?"

He shrugged. "Sort of."

"You must be really special. I'm not surprised. Of course, you are. You've certainly defied everything I've ever known. Has he ever said why you?"

Evan looked up at the ceiling, noticing for the first time that it was painted like the sky with pale blue and white iridescent clouds. Had Jazmine done this? How had he not noticed this yesterday? There was a bit of yellowish-orange spreading from the west of the ceiling, mimicking the sun rising, and a flock of blackbirds were painted on the ceiling in the far east. She was very talented.

Well, now he liked her even more. "Yeah, he said he had a gut feeling that I was more than I appeared. I feel like I've been letting him down. I'm just a bartender, but he still has faith in me. I don't want to be anything more than I am, though. I just want to be left alone. Most of the time, I'm still the kid in the woods who didn't want to be bothered with people when they found me. Except you. I like being with you. Wait, that didn't make sense."

Jazmine chuckled and snuggled up closer to him. "Yes, it does. And as for your specialness, aren't you curious to find out why you're so different?"

He shrugged. "I used to, but not anymore. Even with you, I don't think I care. I'm just happy for now."

She gave him a slight squeeze, which he took way too much happiness from. No, he really didn't care about the whys anymore. That just brought drama, and he preferred a much simpler existence. Which is why he really didn't want to go to this club. There would be nothing but drama.

And danger.

CHAPTER 10

*T*he rest of the week was uneventful. Jazmine was a bit embarrassed at how dull a life she lived. She'd never noticed it until Evan had arrived. She'd never really cared that she rarely left her apartment. It was just the way things were. But with him there, she could feel how stilted her life had become. She worried that he was bored, but he never showed it. Instead, he cooked, he read books, he explored the town. He seemed truly content. And after work, they spent all their time together. They played games, ate, watched movies, and walked around late at night.

They still slept together every night, but she kept it PG. All she wanted was his touch. She feared doing anything more because when he left, she'd feel that void. Kissing, at least from what she'd seen in movies, seemed to be way too intimate and hold way too much emotion. She was already weary of getting too used to lying beside him, but she told herself she deserved that bit of happiness for just a short while.

When Saturday came, her were nerves scrambled. In part, because she was nervous about her mission, which her scrimpy one-week training did little to soothe, and also because that meant that Evan was leaving soon. He had to make a living after all, and he couldn't stay here. That would only draw suspicion. Whatever fake background he had concocted was strong enough to withstand her sister's search so on that he was safe, but his ruse couldn't last forever. This was possibly their last night together.

When she stepped out of her bedroom that night, she found Evan on the couch, resting his arms on his thighs, waiting for her. His eyes grew wide when he saw her, and he stood up.

She looked down at herself, suddenly feeling very self-conscious. Matt, who worked in one of the local clothing boutiques, had come over with outfits, accessories and make-up, and had instructed Paige on how to apply her make-up from a careful distance. He'd always seemed unafraid of her power, but he was no fool either, and that night, she had only her protective gloves to mute her magic.

Of all the outfits she tried on, the least offensive to her more conservative fashion sense was a red, mid-calf satin slip dress with a slit that came below her knees. She added an ankle-length cardigan as flimsy coverage against someone accidentally bumping into her. She paired her outfit with a choker and black combat boots. Her hair was pulled up in a high bun with select tendrils pulled down to frame her face. Paige gave her a smoky eye to complete the look, a face of disapproval set the entire time she was there. Jazmine fought back the urge to remind her sister that it was her fiancé who put her in this mess.

When Jazmine looked in the mirror, she instantly thought of the women in old movies she'd seen. When she'd tried to wrap a plaid shirt around her waist, Matt had insisted she not. He was still glaring at her choice of footwear, but she'd refused to put on the knee-high boots he'd offered. They didn't look comfortable or running appropriate if she had to escape.

"Do I look okay?" she asked, wrapping her arms around herself.

Evan just stared at her with lips slightly parted before blinking his eyes several times and nodding. "Yes, you look amazing. You look beautiful."

She smiled shyly and looked away. He seemed to be genuine when he complimented her, and the look in his eyes made her stomach flutter. Jazmine decided that Evan had the best eyes. They could pierce her soul if she stared long enough. "You don't look so bad yourself."

He snorted. "I look like I need to change."

He wore dark jeans stuffed into brown boots, a fitted, untucked white button-down shirt and a tie. Jazmine thought he looked handsome with his tousled hair. He looked like a model in an old teen magazine. She was going to miss him.

"When are you leaving?" As soon as she asked the question, she realized how it sounded.

The hurt look on his face clearly conveyed that he took it the wrong way.

"No, it's only that, I really like having you here. I'm going to miss you when you leave."

"I honestly don't *want* to go back." He scratched his head. "I guess I'll know after tonight. I have to make sure they don't keep sending you on these dangerous missions. I want to be here to protect you if they do."

"It's not your job to protect me."

He nodded slowly, pressing his lips together in thought before he finally spoke. "I know it's not. But I can't help but want to. I think you'll have to deal with it." He smirked at her,

She opened her mouth to protest, but someone knocked at the door.

She went to the door and looked through the peephole. Bryant stood there without Paige. Now what could he want? She sucked in a breath and then opened the door. "Hi, Bryant. What's going on?"

He gave her his usual politician fake smile and strolled past her into the apartment.

"Come on in," she muttered.

"Just thought I'd come by before you left to give you a good pep talk. I know you're probably nervous." He looked around her apartment. He wiped a finger on a bookshelf in the living room and looked at the dust on his finger before brushing his hands together.

Jazmine didn't see Evan, and she assumed he had gone to the bedroom. She didn't blame him for leaving.

"You know, I like you, Jazmine." Bryant turned toward her. "You're a good girl with an unfortunate magic. I used to think it would be best to keep you locked up for the safety of our town, but maybe you can be useful."

She crossed her arms. "I'm already useful."

He gave her a condescending smile. "Of course you are, making games and all that. But I mean really useful. Maybe do something that can actually help society as a whole. Like removing difficult people."

She didn't like the sound of that. Did he want her to be some kind of hitman? "What are you getting at?"

He gave a shrug. "Maybe we should have had you join our military force. There are a lot of dangerous people in the world, and you have a gift that can work fast. Maybe we should develop your powers more. You don't know all that you can do. Maybe you poison food a target eats. Maybe you don't have to even touch a person to kill them. You could just use your mind. Have you tried?" He levitated an old DVD off of her coffee table. "Your sister's powers have grown. Why not yours?"

While it was true Paige could increase the strength of

healing potions and medicines, there was no way that Jazmine was going to try such a thing herself. Her test subjects wouldn't get helped. They'd die. And in what world would she want to do mass killings anyway? "I'm not an assassin."

He gave a light chuckle. "You sure about that?" He psychically floated a book into an open space in the bookshelf.

She put her hand on her hip. "Is there anything else you wanted?"

He turned to her and grinned. "Do a good job tonight. And when the time is right, maybe we can test how great that magic of yours is." He then walked away without saying goodbye, leaving Jazmine standing in her living room, shaking with anger.

~

Seduction was exactly as she imagined it would be from all her years of watching old movies and TV shows where there was a sexy club scene. It was located in the downtown area of D.C on a very unbusy street that looked like it once had been a popular location for dining and clubs. There was no line outside or even a sign since it was exclusive and members only. From the outside, it looked like a large yet closed restaurant. Jazmine couldn't even hear music, and there was no doorman.

As soon as the pair reached the door, it opened automatically, and they stepped into a pitch-black space. A booming voice came from somewhere unknown and asked for a special password, which Jazmine gave. Then another door opened, letting them see dim lighting and hear loud house music.

The space was dark with warm yellow lights scattered about. Black walls and dark hardwood floors set with elegant, gold-framed artwork and leather and suede seating completed the look. A long glass bar and mirrored ceiling added the final touches, giving the room a vibe of a grand speakeasy.

A woman dressed in a skimpy black dress welcomed them with a smile and requested payment, which would cover two drinks each and the experience, whatever that entailed. If they wanted to go beyond the drink limit, they could come back to her to provide additional payment.

"Is this your first time?" she asked, batting long eyelashes.

Jazmine nodded her head, tentatively. She was suddenly very nervous.

As if sensing her unease, Evan reached out for her hand. She was thankful Evan was with her. She didn't think she could do this alone. There were way too many people there, and she was highly uncomfortable.

"Would you like a guide or a map?" the hostess asked, glancing between the both of them.

"Why do we need that?" Jazmine replied.

"Well, this place is deceptively large, and the rooms outside of the main club spaces on this and the second floor have different themes or uses. There are donation rooms, strictly for the sharing of energy and blood. Then, there are rooms that exchange a bit...more." Her eyes rested on Evan when she said the last part, but he looked unbothered.

"More?" Jazmine scrunched her face up. "You mean sex?" Why did people have to be so mysterious? Did they think it was sexy? It wasn't. She just wanted people to say exactly what they meant.

The hostess gave a light chuckle. "Yes, sweetie. All kinds, depending on the room. There are also viewing rooms if you just like to watch." The hostess gave her a map and smiled slightly at Jazmine, assessing her.

Jazmine had been a voyeur all her life, but this was not

what she wanted to be doing right now, especially with Evan by her side. What had her people sent her here to do? Her face flushed, and she thanked the woman before moving away, almost bumping into a male waiter.

She stopped and let out a breath. *Calm down, Jazmine. Do not let these people trip you up before you can finish this mission.* If she didn't get anything tonight, she was going to have to come back, and she really didn't want that. Yet, after her talk with Bryant, she wasn't so sure she'd have a choice. She was still thrown off by his visit.

Evan had looked murderous after Bryant left, matching her own mood. "You've never been to a club, right?" Evan asked in her ear, his breath touching her skin and sending a welcomed shiver through her.

"I've never been anywhere normal outside the grocery store and the library."

"They really set you up with this one. Couldn't send you to just a regular club." He shook his head, agitation on his face.

"You said you've been here before?"

He looked away, his face slightly flushed. "Yeah, for the blood donations only, though." He looked back at her with shameful eyes.

She gave his hand a light squeeze. "It's okay. You're a vampire. I understand."

"I try to only drink the blood of animals, normally."

"I know. It's okay, Evan." She couldn't forget what he was. He had special needs that many other paranormals didn't have. She'd be foolish to think that he wouldn't want to partake in human blood from time to time. It was her understanding that it was tastier than animal blood, and apparently, paranormal blood was the most delicious.

She looked around the space, noticing for the first time some of her town's police force scattered about the space with eyes on her. A man dressed in all black gave her a curt nod, and she turned away, finding little comfort with the added protection. She really just wanted to get in and get out.

They headed to the bar and ordered a drink. Jazmine took a long gulp of her dark liquor. It had a slightly sweet taste, and she decided she really enjoyed it. She wondered if she could get a bottle of it for the way home. *Stay focused, lady,* she scolded herself. "Okay. They told us to stick to the club spaces and small group areas. Others are going to the one on one rooms." She felt a tiny relief in that. Maybe the attackers would just grab people out of the private rooms. Less conspicuous, although clandestine didn't seem to be their M.O. recently.

Damn, she wasn't ready for this. She was going to mess this up and get someone killed.

~

*E*van looked over to Jazmine and watched her take another swig of her drink until it was gone. If she continued to drink that fast, she was going to be too drunk to be of any use. She continued to look around the room as if waiting for something to happen. She looked like a nervous first-timer, which in a way made her more approachable to someone up to no good, but he also didn't want her making herself sick.

He put an arm around her waist and drew her to him. "You're going to be okay. I'm not going to let anyone hurt you." Damn, she smelled good. She had on a different scent tonight, something flowery that made him feel like he was walking through a rose garden. It sped up his heart. His wonderful, still-beating heart.

But it also made him drop fang. This environment wasn't

helping. He could smell the scent of blood all around him. Blood and sex. That, coupled with the liquor, and he was far from his most in-control. Still, he had to pull it together if he was going to watch out for Jazmine.

How was he going to leave her if he was her protector now? Jasper had already sent him an email two days ago. It was a simple one-liner. *How are things?* A simple question that demanded an in-depth answer, and Jasper wasn't asking about how he was enjoying the trip. He wanted information that could help him against possible enemies.

Evan waited a full day before responding and had just provided general information about their suspicions regarding the attacks and the town's general structure and defenses. Really nothing they didn't already know.

Jasper had replied with one word. *Interesting.*

Evan was no fool. Nothing he'd written was interesting. Jasper believed he was holding out. The longer Evan stayed, the more Jasper would be expecting. He'd have to leave soon.

"This place is really popular, huh?" Jazmine said to the bartender, a bald man with a tattoo that wrapped around his scalp.

Evan blinked and focused on their mission. This was not the time to get lost in thought.

The bartender nodded. "Yeah, it's not that busy tonight, though. Might be because of the attacks going on," he stated, pouring her drink into her short glass.

"Have there been attacks at any bars and clubs?"

"I heard of one across town. The kidnappers came on a dead night and took everyone out the whole damn place." Seeing the alarm on Jazmine's face, the bartender threw out a hand. "But don't worry. This place is safe. You can't just come in without knowing someone and getting the password, and this place is warded so no teleporting in or out."

"Have you heard anything else about these attacks?" Jazmine put a hand on her chest. "I mean, it's really scary."

Evan knew she was acting helpless and afraid to strengthen her role as bait material, but he still wanted to reach out and grab her hand.

The bartender agreed before excusing himself to service another customer.

"I heard that they steal people and use them as sex slaves," said a woman standing beside Evan. She was older with blond hair that reached her waist. Her glassy eyes made it clear to Evan that she was already well into intoxication. "My, aren't you handsome?" She trailed a finger down his arm. "Are you a vampire? I like to donate."

Jazmine grabbed his other arm and yanked him near her. "Sorry. He's taken." She moved them away from the bar, and they left the main club area through the back hall, which led to stairs and other closed rooms. Was she jealous or just playing the role? Evan hoped it was the former.

They walked down the hall towards an open door leading to the outside, her hand still on his arm. They entered a large courtyard full of greenery, cobblestone, fairy lights and seating. Music from inside transmitted outside through speakers. People sat and stood about the space, smoking hookah, drinking, donating blood, or kissing.

Evan inhaled the deep aroma of blood. Blood was an interesting substance. It all smelled the same, but the taste was very different. However, it all made his mouth water.

"Do you want to get out of here?" Jazmine asked, looking at him with worry.

He covered his still protruding incisors and shook his head.

She reached up and removed his hand, staring at his teeth.

"Sorry," he said in a low voice. "I'm not going to—"

"Hurt me," she finished and nodded. "I know. Our first night together, you drank my blood, but you didn't overdrink, even though you were injured. I'm not worried. Do you need blood now?"

He looked away, suddenly embarrassed. "Not from you." He ran his fingers through his hair, his hand trembling slightly. "I didn't mean that how it sounded. You just aren't my donor. Never think you are. If I need blood, I'll do my best to get it on my own. I don't want to take from you again."

She touched his arm. "The bar out here looks like they sell blood. Go grab a drink."

They headed to the bar, and he ordered a sweet blood, feeling more than self-conscious as Jazmine watched him over the rim of her own drink at her lips. He turned slightly away from her to drink, and she didn't move to try to look. In fact, she seemed unbothered and more at ease as the evening moved on.

Two hours passed without incident. They explored more of the club, seeing sights that made him more than uncomfortable.

Jazmine, on the other hand, seemed totally fascinated. In a way, that was good. It made her more relaxed and less nervous.

They made their way back to the courtyard bar, and Evan hoped they could call it a night. The mission wasn't a success, which didn't bother him except for the fact that the town would probably send Jazmine out again if this failed.

He felt a tap on his shoulder and turned slightly. A dark-haired man with a mustache and dead red eyes stood behind. "Do you share?" he asked in a gruff voice.

"Excuse me?" Evan replied with raised brows.

He swayed slightly in his stance, seemingly drunk. "Your woman. Do you share? Do you let others take from her?" His voice sounded slurred. Definitely drunk.

Jazmine, overhearing the exchange, leaned past Evan and glared at the man. "Why are you asking him?"

The mustache man gave her a tight-lipped smile. "Because I want to avoid trouble."

"She's her own person," Evan replied stiffly. He wanted to shove this guy in the chest and get him away from her. However, that wasn't part of the plan since she was bait.

The man looked to her. "I pay well."

Before he could punch the guy, a scream interrupted their exchange, and Evan turned to his left as a woman grabbed another lady by the shoulder. At first, he thought it was the attackers but soon realized it was a catfight over a third woman over who got to drink from her.

He rolled his eyes. He really hated this place.

"Let go," Jazmine shouted.

He turned back around and found Jasmine pulling back from the man with the mustache, who had a firm hold on her gloved wrist.

"Let her go!" Evan shouted, shoving the man in the chest, but he kept his grip on Jazmine.

The man started to fade out.

Shit, he was trying to teleport. If he left, he'd be taking Jazmine with him.

How? Evan thought this place was warded. That should have also included the courtyard. The ward had to be broken.

Evan punched the man in the head and pulled at the hand gripping Jazmine. No luck, he was like stone. The man backhanded Evan, sending him to the ground.

"Evan," Jazmine cried. She gripped her free hand onto the bar counter, her face a mask of fear. "Unglove me!"

That's right. She wouldn't be able to kill the attacker if she couldn't get her gloves off.

"He can't help you," the man sneered. More of his body began to fade away from the ground up, and for the first time, Evan noticed that Jasmine was also fading. They were both now floating bodies with no legs. In seconds they would be fully gone.

Evan shot up and lunged forward. He grabbed Jazmine's free hand and pulled off the glove in one swift movement, and she slapped the man across the face with her bare hand.

The man kept his hand around Jazmine's wrist as she pushed her hand into the base of his throat, holding contact. Evan punched him in the back of his head again, sending the man falling on his butt and releasing his gripe.

Jazmine stumbled forward, tipping over, but Evan grabbed her by the arm and pulled her back towards him.

The man retched a thick black substance. More of the goo poured from his mouth and nose before he collapsed on the ground, dead.

The hairs on the back of Evan's neck stood at attention, and he spun around, his vampire nails growing, and swung out at a woman who tackled him to the ground. Her eyes were also red, and she opened her mouth, impossibly wide, to bite him. However, his talons had connected with her stomach, and he twisted his hand, causing her to jump off of him. She hunched forward, grabbing her stomach and hissing at him.

Jazmine raced to her and slapped the woman's forehead.

Soon after, the vampire dropped to the ground in seizures, black goo oozing from her mouth and spilling from her wound in her stomach before dying.

Three other red-eyed vampires appeared around them.

Jazmine dropped her shoulders. "I can't kill anymore," she said in an unsteady voice, her eyes dulling.

Evan jumped up. He wouldn't have her kill anymore, either. Where the hell was security and backup? He raced toward one of the vampires closest to her and tackled him to the ground. From his peripheral vision, he could finally see security and Jazmine's horrible backup appear to take down the other attacking vampires.

The male vampire he battled took a bite out of his shoulder.

Evan punched the man in the side of his head in rapid succession. His knuckles soon bled, but the vampire kept biting into his shoulder as if he didn't know he was being hit. However, Evan could see he was doing clear damage to the vampire's head as the skin split and bloodied.

"Evan!" Jazmine shouted. "You're disappearing!"

He looked down, and for the first time, noticed only his upper body was visible. Both his lower body and the lower body of his attacker were now gone. Not good.

He struggled to get away from the vampire, but he had wrapped his arms around Evan, holding tightly. Evan pulled away, and the vampire's teeth tore at his shoulder. The man squeezed even tighter, constricting the air in Evan's lungs.

How strong was this guy? Evan thought himself a pretty strong vampire until this moment. He couldn't even wiggle out of this guy's grasp.

Jazmine ran towards them, but a gun appeared at the skull of the vampire, shooting. The vampire instantly died, and the teleportation stopped, returning both their bodies. Evan rolled off the vampire and let out a thankful sigh. He looked up at one of the undercover officers, a woman with short blond hair, and nodded a thanks.

Jazmine soon appeared at his side, checking his body for wounds. "Your shoulder," she whispered.

"It's a scratch. It'll heal quick," he replied. "Are you okay?"

She nodded, but her eyes seemed distant. "I'll live. How did they get in? This place is warded."

Evan sat up, wincing at the pain from his wound. "They obviously knew the password."

"Wards can only do so much," stated the female officer who'd shot the vampire. "We'll take it from here."

Yeah, now that Jazmine and Evan had done most of the hard work. *Useless, all of them.*

He looked over to Jazmine. She looked scared. Her normally stoic demeanor was now replaced with fear. She hunched slightly and wrapped her arms around her body as she stared down at the ground. She was not all right, and he couldn't leave her. Not anytime soon.

Jasper would have to wait.

CHAPTER 11

The ride home from the club was a blur. Jazmine knew she was leaving the club and that Evan was driving them back. She knew they'd made it back to her apartment, but she couldn't tell exactly how she'd left. She hadn't spoken since she killed two attackers.

She'd killed someone.

Again.

In just one moment, she'd doubled the amount of lives she'd taken. She was only nineteen. At this rate, she could kill hundreds of people before she died of old age.

It had been the plan to kill one person, but she hadn't been prepared for how it would feel. She didn't even kill anyone at the bazaar attack, although she was ready. Or so she thought. No, she would never be ready to kill. Even if the people she killed were bad, she couldn't will herself to feel okay with it. But did that justify killing them? Was that the equal punishment?

She walked straight to her room and collapsed on the bed. She didn't think she'd be able to sleep even though she was exhausted.

Evan laid down behind her. He wrapped an arm around

her stomach and pulled her to him. "Do you want to talk?" he asked, his breath tickling her neck.

She liked that feeling. "No." Talking was bad. Talking was depressing, and she was tired. So tired and yet too scared to sleep. She'd only see the faces of the lives she took in mind. "No talking. I just want you to touch me." She grasped his hands around her waist and slowly moved them up to her breast.

He stiffened for a moment before she felt his hands begin to massage her. Her body relaxed, her core coming to life. She'd never felt anything like this. Never in any of her dreams. She pressed her lips together to hold in a moan as his fingers found her nipples. She crossed her legs, sure she would explode if he continued.

She turned to find his lips and kissed him. She enjoyed the feel of his lips and his taste. There was a bitter sweetness to his skin she enjoyed.

He kissed her harder, careful of his incisors. His tongue darted into her mouth, and she tasted more of him, touching his tongue with her own. Every nerve in her body came to attention, and she briefly wondered if she could feel him come alive.

His hands found her bottom, and he ground her to him. He was excited. She could feel it. Her mind buzzed. Everything hummed. She wanted him. Now. He could make her forget the night.

He pulled back slightly, and she could see his enlarged black pupils, blocking most of the white of his eyes.

She gave him a questioning look.

He sighed, throwing his head back. "If we keep at this, I won't want to stop. Of course, I will. I'm not a monster." He looked back down at her, brushing a strand of hair from her face.

"I don't want you to."

"Yes, you do. You'll regret it. Tonight's not right. I want something more special for you."

She cocked an eyebrow. What could be more special? Candlelight? Mood music? Why did he care? Shouldn't he be excited for this chance? She was sure she hadn't misread all his signs.

She opened her mouth to protest when she heard a knock at the door. She grumbled and sat up.

"It's nearly two in the morning. Do you usually get late-night visitors?" Evan asked, also sitting up.

"Never." She walked to the front door, her heart even heavier than before. Evan did take her attention away from the night, but it also highlighted her growing feelings for him. When he left, it would hurt like hell, and she had done that to herself.

She looked through the peephole and saw her sister's angry face in the hallway. She really didn't feel like dealing with her now.

"It's late, Paige, can you come back tomorrow?" she called through the door.

"No," said a familiar male voice.

She looked back through the hole and saw Theo there.

"Open up, woman, we aren't leaving," he shouted.

She sighed and opened the door. "Why are you both here?" she questioned as they walked inside.

"Because you went on a dangerous mission and then just came back without saying anything," Paige stated, walking to the living room.

Theo looked her up and down. "You look hot. Matt did well."

Evan walked from the bedroom, his shirt disheveled and hair messier than usual.

Theo raised a brow. "Uh, did we interrupt something?" He crossed his arms and smirked at Jazmine, who rolled her eyes.

"What is he doing here?" Paige asked, pointing to Evan. "I thought he was staying in the guest hotel."

Jazmine gave her a wide grin. She really didn't want to hear her sister nag her tonight. "I lied. Not sorry."

Paige let out a long-suffering sigh and rubbed her temples. "Really, Jaz. You are too smart to be this stupid. He's a stranger."

Jazmine's forced smiled turned to a grimace. "A stranger who saved my life tonight. Look, I'm really tired, and he was just keeping me company. You should thank him instead of giving him the stink eye."

Paige looked Evan up and down, eyes still angry. "Thank you," she replied through gritted teeth.

Jazmine gave a smug nod and crossed her arms over her chest. "Now, you can see I'm doing just fine. So, you can go home and tell your fiancé I've earned my keep and to please leave me alone forever."

Paige huffed and put her hands on her hips. "It wasn't like that."

Theo chuckled. "Sure, it wasn't, honey." Theo sat on the couch.

Evan took a seat next to him.

"Well, don't you want to know what they found out when the necromancer brought the attackers back to life for questioning? And before you ask, they sent them back to death. The ones you…disposed of can't be reanimated for long. Your poisoning gift is a doozy."

Jazmine shrugged and sat at her dining room table. "Sure."

"Bryant stated that this cult is actually some organized crime gang."

"What are they doing?" Theo asked. "Kidnapping people to use them as slaves for labor or sex?"

Paige nodded. "That and more. They kidnap not just paranormals but regular immune humans too. Apparently, there are various things the paranormals are used for, but the one unique thing they want paranormals for is their blood. Although human blood is sold as well, paranormal blood has healing properties, and as we've been hearing, humans have been using it to make some form of serum to give them super powers."

Theo shook his head. "I'm sure that's worth a lot. Regular humans have been pissed they didn't get powers for a while now. If they want to eat brains for a living, have at it. Right?" Theo elbowed Evan, who gave him a questioning look.

Jazmine held her breath, hoping he hadn't forgotten that he was supposed to be a zombie right now.

Evan gave a lopsided smile and nodded.

"We don't have it so bad," Paige replied.

Theo scoffed. "We all can't be beautiful healers like you."

Paige threw her hands out to the side and sat down at the dining table. "I'm just saying, I can see why there's a market for our blood. Life must be hard without magic. Especially if you live in one of those humans-only towns. No electricity, no cars. They're practically living in the dark ages just to prove a point."

"Anything else you learned?" Jazmine asked, leaning an elbow on the table. The adrenaline of the night was beginning to wear off, and she was starting to feel very tired.

"Well, the gang is all vampires," Paige answered. "There are other crime units involved in this trade as well but the ones attacking in this area are a vampire only gang."

Jazmine fought hard not to look over to Evan. Could they be from his town? Did he secretly know about them, and he never said anything? She didn't believe that. He'd looked out for her so well so far. Maybe he honestly didn't know about the crime coming from his town.

Paige continued, "So, there is thought that the vampire town in D.C. might be housing this group either knowingly or unknowingly."

"They could be from any town. Or no town," Evan offered, adjusting in his seat.

Jazmine narrowed her eyes at Evan. Now he was trying to take attention away from his town. Could he really have known already? She would have to ask them after everyone left.

"It could be, but the attackers said the gang is located near us, although no one would say where exactly." Paige huffed. "So, we're going to be reaching out to the town leadership."

Jazmine tapped her nose in thought. "It's odd that it would be vampires. They don't teleport."

Paige nodded. "Yeah, they got a little help by some witch cohorts. Like I said, this is an operation that just doesn't stop with them. They're just the ones who threaten us in particular."

Jazmine frowned and gnawed her lower lip. Something wasn't right. "It took the vampire who tried to grab me a while to teleport us out. Same with the one who'd tried to take Evan."

"That was a good thing," Evan stated, somberly. "That let us stop him and for you to take him out."

"Okay, but at the bazaar, they were teleporting in and out in a flash."

"The club was warded. It probably slowed down his ability to get out quickly."

Theo crossed his arms and sighed. "Do you think the vampire town is going to work with us? Even if they aren't supporting this group, the last thing they would want is to be housing some gang taking out their neighbors. Towns are going to riot and take them out. Most people already don't like an all-vampire town. I could see them hiding the truth and wanting to deal with it in their own way."

Paige yawned, waving a hand in her face.

Jazmine held in a sigh. They'd gotten all the information

she cared about. She was fine with Paige and Theo leaving now.

Paige rolled her shoulders back showing no signs of leaving. "Bryant thinks we should build an alliance with the vampire town, but the governor doesn't agree. A government town connecting with an all-vampire town, it's unheard of."

Jazmine pffted. "Everything's unheard of nowadays. But I agree that going in there with all our knowledge, accusing a town that has never been harmed by this won't exactly get us Friend of the Year." She shrugged. "It's an interesting dilemma. Oh, well." This wasn't her lane, and if she stayed in the safety of her apartment, then it would stay that way. She'd done as much as she needed to do to be left alone, and as far as she was concerned, there was no more to discuss.

She let out a loud yawn and stretched her arms over her head to give a signal to the group that it was time to leave.

"If you want to learn the truth, you should send a spy in," Evan stated, resting his elbows on his thighs.

Jazmine closed her eyes and let out a sigh. What the hell was this man talking about? Why couldn't he let things be? This was not her lane, or really anyone's in this room. Why couldn't they stay out of it?

Paige nodded thoughtfully, putting a finger to her chin. "Yes. They want to do that, but getting a new vampire in at this time would be very suspicious, especially if the governor insists on questioning the town."

"I could do it," Evan replied in a calm tone.

Jazmine lowered her forehead to the table. What was wrong with this guy? They'd had a really good thing going. Now, here he was, giving away his secret to the soon to be wife of the deputy governor. She never saw Evan as the smartest guy, but she didn't think he was an idiot either. Her sister would never forgive her for covering this up. Neither would Theo. She would have to play this cool. They were the only two people in her life, and she really didn't want to alienate them.

She rested her chin on the table and looked over to Evan. "You aren't a vampire, so how would that work?"

"Or is he?" Theo countered, adjusting on the sofa to face Evan. "You never smelled like the undead to me. There was always something off about you." He squinted his eyes and leaned in towards Evan. "Zombie recognizes zombie, and you ain't looking too familiar, *mi hermano.*"

Evan sat up straight and ran a hand through his hair. "That's because I'm not. I'm a vampire."

Jazmine shot upright. "You're a what?" she cried, touching her chest in mock disbelief.

Evan looked at her with wide eyes and then nodded, seeming to catch on to her ruse. "Yes. I'm sorry I lied. I didn't want to scare you. I just wanted to be close to you."

Theo scrunched his face up. "By being a zombie? You didn't want to be a fairy or something?"

Paige's eyes blazed with anger. "You lied to my sister!" She turned to Jazmine. "See, I told you that you couldn't trust him. You are so gullible."

Theo waved a hand. "Settle down now, mama bear. He didn't hurt her, and he's *trying* to help."

Paige sucked her teeth and looked at Evan with distain. "What else have you lied about? This isn't a game. Tell us everything."

Evan licked his lips and nodded, clasping his hands together like a remorseful child. "I'm from the vampire town. I got a fake ID to come here to see Jaz."

Jazmine jumped to her feet and put her hands to her cheeks. "Oh, my goodness. How could you?" Okay, now this guy was really losing his mind. Didn't he know what would happen if people found out that there were fake IDs and even profiles in the government town systems? Maybe they knew, but it would look really poorly on this town with him getting through.

Paige looked like she might faint, her face draining of color. "I can't believe this. Do you know what could happen to you, to us, for letting you in here? My sister vouched for you! We're in the governor's circle. This could ruin Bryant's career."

"Your sister didn't know."

Paige slapped her hand down on the table, causing Jazmine to jump slightly. "It won't matter, you idiot. People will think you're a spy. You probably are, and we'll be linked in as traitors. It'll be guilt by association. They might kick her out of town. And I can't have her out there on her own. Especially now. So, I'll have to go too. Everything we've worked toward for the past several years here will be gone, flushed down the drain. You are so selfish." Her voice jumped an octave as she bordered on hysterics.

Jazmine needed to take control of this situation. "Paige, we can figure this out." Jazmine sat closer to her sister. "Evan says he can help, so let's hear what he has to say. Let's make this right for you."

Paige glared at her sister then over to Evan. "Well, speak then." She rested her cheek on a fist, her elbow balanced on the table.

Evan nodded. "Right, so I go back home, and I gather any information I can about this vampire crime unit. I can share it with you. I won't tell anyone back home. It hasn't been a threat to us until the bazaar, so someone might let something slip."

Theo tapped his nose with his finger. "It sounds like a plausible plan. But how do we know we can trust you? For all we know, you could have been here this entire time collecting information for your town and with Jaz so close to leadership, she'd be an easy mark. So, you go home and disappear into the wind, telling us nothing. Or you feed us a bunch of garbage."

Evan shrugged. "All that could be true. Even though it's not, I get how you wouldn't trust me. But what if someone came back with me to keep an eye on me and do some reconnaissance themselves?"

"Like who? Another vampire?" Paige asked, eyelids half lowered. She looked like she was falling asleep, but Jazmine was smart enough to know better. She was trying to calm herself to keep from exploding. She'd seen Paige do this before.

"That or maybe Jaz?" Evan gave a sheepish smile.

Jazmine widened her eyes as she looked back at Paige's face.

Paige's own eyes grew large, but she remained still. "Tell me how putting my little sister into a lion's den makes sense?"

"Well, she'll have her touch as a defense and me. Plus, my family knows I like her and wanted to meet her. It won't be odd to have her come back with me for a visit just like I did here. I can even tell people she's a donor, but I won't drink her blood." He rushed out the last part upon seeing Paige stir.

"And did your family expect you to share anything you learned here?"

Evan lifted a shoulder. "I'm sure, but all I have to share is how great this town is and the fact that the attacks are still happening. I didn't learn anything I wasn't supposed to."

Paige twisted her lips. "How fortunate for us."

"I think it's a great idea," Jazmine stated. She actually did *not* think it was a great idea. It would only put her in further harm's way and even more out of her very comfortable, very insulated lane. However, it did mean more time with Evan, and if she did nothing to smooth this situation out, her sister would never let her live it down. She'd been so caught up in Evan that she wasn't thinking practically.

"It's too dangerous," Paige stated, sitting back in her chair.

Jazmine looked down at her hands, which sat in fists on her lap. "Yeah, but someone sent me out to a club to act as bait, and I handled my own just fine without the help of any police force here. Evan has proven he has my back. I know you don't trust him, but I do. Let me be useful again. I may not have another chance to do good. Maybe this kind of stuff *is* my purpose, like healing is yours."

Paige jutted her chin out. "You *have* a purpose. To make computer stuff."

Jazmine rolled her eyes. "I can do more."

Theo scratched his chin in thought. "Maybe this would be good for you. I won't need to force you to leave all the time. You went from add and subtraction to Calculus in one quick jump, but maybe that's okay. You got a lot of life to live, and this small place or some lonely cabin by the lake can't be it for you."

"But it's safer that way," Paige countered with a frown.

"It's boring that way," Theo shot back.

Paige slapped her hand on the table. "She's not your sister."

He gave Paige a soft smile. "She's my best friend and her own person. She's nineteen now. Let the bird out of her cage."

Paige sat back and was quiet for several seconds. She looked at Theo, then Jazmine, then Evan. "I'll see about getting it all cleared for her to go with you. I'll have to modify the story, of course, so we don't look like we got played." She stood up, still angry. "Don't go anywhere until you hear back from me." She looked down at Jazmine. "If you die doing this, I will kill you. And I know that doesn't make sense, but so what?" She pointed a finger at Evan. "You better watch her like your life depends on it because it does."

Theo clapped his hands, getting ready to leave. "Hey, look at the bright side. At least we know that Jaz can touch undead vampires without killing them. So, more options in the world for her to date. Sorry, Evan." He patted him on the shoulder.

Jazmine bit her lip. There was no need for her to tell them how she'd actually brought Evan back to life at that moment. That would just be a distraction. However, at some point, she would have to tell her sister the whole truth, and she knew there would be a scalpel with Evan's name on it when the time came.

CHAPTER 12

*E*van smiled into Jazmine's wide-eyed expression as
he gave her a tour of his town several days later. His
community was small but upscale, having taken over the
high-end Georgetown area of D.C. The main street was still
lined with various restaurants and upscale shops,
surrounded by the Potomac River and beautiful brownstone
houses. The area was once highly desirable until it became
infested by gremlins and ghosts, and the river inhabited by
some sort of magical piranhas.

The prior citizens had fled the area amongst the Sickness
and the supernatural chaos. Vampires had come in later,
killing and running out the gremlins. As for the ghosts,
they'd hired exorcists and witches to remove those. They'd
feasted on and had made a profit selling other towns the
flesh-eating fish.

Others had tried to encroach back in once the proverbial
coast was clear, but Jasper and his growing hunter and police
force had put a stop to any groups that had attempted to
overtake the now ideal location. So far, it was working, and
now people stayed clear of the mostly vampire area except

for a few donors who received special permission to live there.

"Where do you stay?" Jazmine asked, peering into a dress boutique. "This place is so fashionable. I haven't seen one bummy person on the street." She tugged at the bottom of her T-shirt, which was paired with jeans and tennis shoes.

Evan snorted. He hoped she wasn't feeling self-conscious. She was beautiful in anything. "Yeah. Vampires like to dress up even with no place to go. I live in a hotel up the street from the bar I work at. Since it's just me, I don't get a house." Actually, that wasn't the full truth. He *could* get a house because he was Jasper's adopted son, but it seemed wasteful to him. Space was a premium in this area of their community.

"Do you have to work today?" Jazmine asked, nervously clutching her crossbody bag to her as she moved out of the way of an oncoming group of giggling girls.

"No. Tomorrow I do. But I can still show you the bar tonight. We should get you to the hotel so we can put your things up." He rolled her small suitcase behind him as they continued their walk.

She shook her head. "I'm enjoying seeing the area. It looks like it did years ago when I was here with my family on a trip once. It's so normal here. I don't know why I didn't expect it to be. No one looks any different than the folks in my town. Except everyone's really pretty."

Evan chuckled. He touched her back and ushered her to the right, down a side street to his hotel. "A lot of vampires use their glamour magic like the fae. Most of these people aren't as beautiful as you'd think."

She glanced up at him, her mouth in an o shape. "Are you using glamour magic?"

"No." He smirked and grabbed her hand. "So, you think I'm pretty?"

She blushed and looked away, still keeping her hand in

his, which made him happy. He led her inside the stylish boutique hotel he called home. When the vampires had taken over that part of town, work had been put into rejuvenating the area that had been destroyed by the gremlins and left to age and disrepair. He'd actually helped to bring this particular hotel back to its former glory, having picked up construction and carpentry from his grandfather while living in isolation.

"I'm in a suite, but there's only one bed and a separate living area with a couch. You can stay with me, or I can get you a room."

She looked around at the extravagant furniture and artwork and the grand chandelier of the lobby, an expression of awe on her face. "No worries. I can stay with you."

He nodded, pleased with her response. Once they arrived to his place, Jazmine contacted her sister and took a nap.

When she awoke, he took her to dinner at a waterfront seafood restaurant where she tried the flesh-eating magic fried fish and declared it a culinary triumph. It was the first time he was able to eat the fish, thanks to her, and he shared her sentiment.

"Is this a date?" Jazmine asked as they strolled over to his bar after dinner. "Because it feels like a date. I know I'm supposed to be on duty or whatever, but it doesn't seem like work."

Evan chuckled, grabbing her hand again. It felt weird to be near her and not touch her. "Well, I hope hanging out with me isn't work for you. Is it okay that I'm still touching you? I know our deal is done now." He felt a little let down by that. He'd gotten to touch more of her the other night. More than he thought he would.

If her sister and Theo hadn't shown up, he wondered where the night would have gone. It had given him much material the following nights in his dreams. He wondered if it was just the excitement of the night that had made her so bold. He wouldn't pressure her for more, but he wouldn't mind it if she wanted to extend their arrangement.

∼

*J*azmine nodded quickly. "Yes. While I'm here, if you want to continue our set up, then I'd be fine with that." She looked up at him shyly. Of course, she didn't mind. Touching him was the highlight of her recent days. If she was so near to him, why would she stop?

He smiled and seemed to nod to himself. "Good." He stopped walking and turned to her before leaning down, moving her hair to the side, and kissing her neck.

Her neck.

Not her cheek, forehead, or lips. The contact from his full lips sent a jolt to her core. How could such a simple kiss have such an affect? She'd read that the neck could be an erogenous zone, but never could she have fully understood that until now. Her own touch of her neck certainly hadn't awakened her in this way. She suddenly mourned all of the touches and feels she had yet to experience. It seemed they were just scratching the surface.

"Do that again," she whispered, her lids half closed.

Evan smiled and kissed her neck again. His lips lingered on her skin longer this time before moving to her earlobe, where he briefly sucked the thin skin of her ear.

Jazmine's knees practically buckled. Maybe they did because it felt like he was holding her up. That settled it, she was in her own real-life romance novel like so many of her books.

"I can do more of this later," he whispered, his breath sending yet another ripple of delight through her.

Jazmine opened her mouth to reply that later should be

now, and she would be just fine skipping the bar, but a shrill voice called out before she could speak.

"Evan? Is that you?" called the female voice.

Evan swore lightly and pulled slowly away from Jazmine, much to her displeasure. He turned towards the voice. "Thalia, what's up?"

A red-headed woman looked between Evan and Jazmine with sharp blue eyes. Two other women stood by her side. The trio wore skimpy dresses that hugged every curve of their body in the most flattering of ways.

Jazmine wondered if this was what women wore out at night. It was only Thursday, and she didn't think it was a prime partying night, but what did she know? Outside of the night at *Seduction*, she'd never done a night of clubbing. Based on what she'd seen in movies and at *Seduction*, she supposed these beautiful women were dressed appropriately.

The woman named Thalia put a hand on her hip. "What's up with you? Why didn't you tell me you were back from your little trip?"

Who was this woman? She seemed less than pleased to see Jazmine. Was she an ex of Evan's? Or maybe some girl who was hoping to get the cute bartender's attention? She'd seen in movies and read in books how bartenders tended to be ladies' men. Was Evan that kind of guy? Did he go from woman to woman, breaking hearts?

Evan shrugged. "I was just preoccupied." He gave Jazmine's hand a little squeeze.

She tried to fight back a smile. It felt like a victory, but why should she care? Evan wasn't her boyfriend. He was just infatuated with her, and she had just made an arrangement with him. Why should she be jealous if he had other women? He wasn't hers.

"Is this the glorious Jazmine you spoke of?" Thalia asked, assessing her with a cold eye. She clearly was unimpressed.

Jazmine suddenly felt inadequate in her purple halter sundress.

"Yes, it is," Evan replied with a wide grin.

"I'm hardly amazing," she muttered.

"Don't sell yourself short. Jazmine, this is my adopted sister, Thalia. And those are her friends whose names I don't remember."

Thalia rolled her eyes and huffed. "You seemed to have mesmerized my brother. He rarely likes anything, and he does not go out unless he's working or wants to find blood. And here he is taking you out on a date." She wagged a finger at Jazmine. "There are some women who would be very jealous of you. I hope you feel lucky."

Thalia obviously thought Jasmine was lacking and should be counting her lucky stars someone as handsome as Evan had dared glance her way. Or was that all in her head?

"I'm the lucky one," Evan shot back. "Anyway, we're off. I'm going to show her my bar."

"Oh, we'll come too," Thalia exclaimed, clacking over to them in her impossibly high heels. Jazmine would have tripped on her face, but apparently, vampires were great at balance.

Evan sighed. "Shouldn't you be at home sad about your missing best friend?"

Thalia pouted. "Well, she really wasn't my *best* friend. We were more like frenemies."

The other women around her nodded.

"And while it is sad, I'm sure she'd want me to live my best life still."

Evan closed his eyes and shook his head, amazed. "Well, a dive bar isn't exactly your scene. Don't you have some club to stand on a table in?"

Thalia giggled. "We'll go there later. Let's hang with your new friend for a bit. I'm your sister, after all. I should know who you hang out with. Even though you don't know *my* friends."

The two other women cut their eyes at him and grumbled.

Jazmine reined in a sigh. This was not what she wanted. Too many people. Too many chances to accidentally kill someone. She had no idea how this could end well.

~

*T*halia never wanted to hang around with Evan. He knew she was just with them to be annoying, which was her specialty. However, since she'd lost her friend and he'd been helpless to rescue or find the woman, he decided he would be nice and not resist her company. He just hoped it was only for a short period of time.

When they arrived at the bar, it was not yet busy. It was too early for that, and this was what he wanted since he could already feel Jazmine tensing up at the extra company. Crowds were understandably not her thing, but she'd bravely agreed to see where he worked. He also wanted to get her out since he would have to work the next couple of nights, and he didn't want her stuck too many days in the hotel room. Although, he realized how silly that was since staying in was actually her place of comfort.

They ordered drinks at the bar. He tried his best to limit the grilling Thalia was giving Jazmine, but she took it in stride with a smile. However, he just wanted to protect her and keep her to himself. He didn't even want his sister knowing her. He didn't want anyone to taint the perfection that was Jazmine. She had brought him to life, and he just wanted to hold her close and keep her from any harm. Not that Thalia would or could harm her.

After an hour, he asked if she was ready to leave. The bar

was starting to pick up, and it would get crowded even on a Thursday.

"All right, I'm taking Jaz out of here," he announced, giving the bartender a salute.

Thalia grabbed his arm. "Aww, but the night is still young."

Evan gently removed her hands from his arm. "You know this isn't my scene unless I'm working. I just wanted to show Jazmine the place. She's seen it. We can go."

Thalia pouted and looked over to Jazmine. "Do you really want to leave now? I know you're just a human, but we have potions that can keep you up all night just like us."

"She doesn't want any drugs," Evan grumbled.

Thalia smiled. "Jazzy here is a big girl. Let her speak for herself."

Evan tilted his head and looked over to Jazmine, hoping she wanted to leave just as much as he did. He was done sharing her.

Jazmine slid off the barstool. She gave a nod to Thalia and her friends. "Thank you so much for hanging out with us. I'm actually a bit tired today. Maybe we can get together again while I'm here."

Thalia chuckled. "Fine. You're a good girl, I see." She glanced down at Jazmine's glove covered arms and hands. "Maybe we can meet up this weekend and go shopping. If you insist on wearing gloves in this heat, perhaps we can find you something more fashionable. Although whatever you're covering, I'm sure it can be healed with vampire blood. Ask Evan." She gave Jazmine a wink before turning away, her friends following.

Jazmine turned away from her, a smile plastered to her face. "She's fun."

"Not really."

"Kitagawa! You're out and with a lovely lady," Travis cried behind him.

Damn it, why was he running into everyone tonight? This was why he never went out.

Travis placed an arm over Evan's shoulders.

He grimaced, his hands balling into fists at his sides.

"I heard you were out with a new face, even eating, and had to see for myself since you usually shut yourself in like some hermit."

Evan shook Travis off his shoulders and grabbed Jazmine's hand.

"What's your name, lovely?" Travis asked with a wide grin, eyeing Jazmine like his next meal.

Jazmine looked at him with raised brows. "I'm Jazmine, a friend of Evan's from out of town."

Travis leaned forward and sniffed the air surrounding her. "You aren't a vampire. Human? Paranormal? Are you his donor?"

Evan pulled her to him. "Don't ask her questions."

Travis laughed. "There you go again, Kitagawa, being a jerk for no reason. I just want to say hi to your lady friend." He looked to Jazmine and took her other gloved hand. "I'm Travis, head of the hunter force in town, and might I say you are absolutely gorgeous." He lowered his head and kissed her hand.

Evan yanked her back roughly, moving her behind him. Who did this asshole think he was? Jazmine was his. He did *not* share.

Travis leaned back, raising his hands. "Whoa, take it easy. You threw your girl into the bar like some rag doll. That's no way to treat a lady."

Evan turned up his upper lip before looking behind him to see Jazmine stare at him with scared eyes as she rubbed her elbow. "I'm sorry, did I hurt you?" He grabbed her elbow and began to rub it.

Travis walked closer to Jazmine. "You know, you don't have to be treated this way. If you want to donate to a

139

vampire who will treat you like the queen you are, then come find me."

Evan shoved Travis in the chest with his free hand.

Travis stumbled back slightly. "You have problems, Kitagawa," Travis shouted, pointing a finger at him. "I'm just trying to have a good time."

"Don't be a jerk," Thalia whispered, standing back with her friends. "He obviously is protective of her. Good donors are hard to find."

"She's not a donor," Evan roared.

"Then why else are you acting like such a dick?" Travis questioned, taking a step forward.

Evan turned away from Jazmine. "Are you my friend?" he asked Travis. "I don't owe you anything."

Travis gave a sour laugh. "You think I'm going to steal your girl?" Travis licked his lips and looked at Jazmine like he was full of naughty ideas for her. "We'd certainly make a better couple.

Evan bared his fangs and hissed at Travis, who returned the behavior. "I will rip your throat out."

Travis' grin widened. "Please try it."

"Hey," boomed a voice from behind them.

King soon appeared in front of the men, his hands on both of their shoulders. "Back it up. No fighting or ripping out throats in my bar. Take it outside." He glanced at Evan. "Although, don't ruin your night with this lovely woman. Calm down." He gave a gentle smile to Jazmine.

"You need to do something about that psycho," Travis said. "Before I do."

Evan tilted his head. He was so sick of this guy. He needed one opportunity to properly kick his ass. "Is that a threat?"

Travis pushed forward against King's large hand. "Yeah."

"The only psycho here is you. You're a thug. You're probably behind the attacks. Not satisfied with blood you're able to legally scrounge up."

Travis paled and took a small step back. He pointed another finger at him. "That's not my thing, and don't you ever accuse me of that. I'm surprised anyone would ever donate blood to you. If anyone's kidnapping people, it'd be you."

"Go take a walk, Travis," King said in a stern voice.

Travis looked up at him as if he planned to argue, but something in King's eyes must have made him nervous because he suddenly looked like someone had let the air out of his tire. He turned on his heel quickly and walked to another part of the bar.

"I don't even know why he keeps coming here," Evan grumbled.

"Put your fangs back. You're scaring her," King ordered, tilting his head towards Jazmine.

Evan touched his mouth. He didn't even realize they were out. He closed his eyes and retracted them before looking over to Jazmine, who had her arms wrapped around herself. He reached out for her.

She took a hesitant step back. "Your eyes are red," she said in a soft voice.

King leaned into him. "Turn around and get yourself together, son."

Evan did as he was told as he tried to calm his nerves so that he could return to normal. What was wrong with him? He was never the think before you act type of guy, but he was smarter than this. He had no reason to think Travis would really try to hurt Jazmine, and he didn't honestly believe she would take off with him. Not that she was his to keep anyway. He was growing too attached to her, and it was making him irrational. If they hadn't even known each other two weeks and he was behaving this way, what would he be like later own? He had to get control of himself. Of his temper.

He breathed slowly, trying to steady his racing heart.

"Jazmine, right?" King asked.

"Yes," she answered.

"I'm King. Evan's boss and failed mentor. I try to keep his temper in check, but it doesn't always work as I'm sure you know by now."

No, she wouldn't know because she hadn't seen him angry. To her, he was just a slightly abnormal guy who had fallen hard for her. He was not a hot-tempered fighter everyone else knew him to be. It was a mistake to bring her here. The more she found out about him, the less she would like him. He would lose her.

King continued. "He's a good guy, and it's evident that he wears his heart on his sleeve. He likes you a lot. Don't let his hot temper scare you off."

Evan turned slightly to her, and his heart sank. King's talk was doing no good. He could see in her eyes, the thing he never wanted to see on her face. Fear.

CHAPTER 13

*J*azmine lay on the bed, looking up at the ceiling while Evan sat in the separate living space, claiming he wasn't tired. He was still upset over the fight, although she thought King had done a good job controlling the situation. Was he mad with her for being scared at the bar? Evan's eyes never did return to their normal color, and she'd tried her best to tell him she didn't fear him but the situation. Vampires fighting was not on her list of things to see in life.

She never knew he was hot-bloodied or quick to start a fight. He seemed exasperated by everyone other than her and King. He seemed to have such patience with her that before tonight she couldn't even imagine him angry. Was it really only because she had made his heart literally beat again? When that infatuation wore off, would he treat her the same way? No, she didn't believe that. She couldn't shake the feeling of trust for him.

She got off the bed and walked to the entrance of the living area. Evan was still lying down on the couch, an arm over his eyes.

"You okay?" she asked, clasping her hands behind her back.

They hadn't really talked on the way home. Comforting people was something she had no experience in, and he kept apologizing to her for being rough when he moved her out of the way. She wasn't sure how many times she had to say that it was okay, even though it was not, and she had every intent on kicking him the next time he got too violent when the situation didn't call for it. However, she tried to let him know that she wasn't mad at him, but he seemed insistent on maintaining his anger at himself.

He pushed his other hand out to stop her. "Don't come closer. I really don't want you to see me like this."

"What? Your red eyes? You won't hurt me. If you thought that you'd have stayed somewhere else."

"You're scared of me."

"I'm not scared. I'm concerned." She walked over to him and pulled at his arm covering his face.

He struggled against her. Darn, he was strong.

She used both hands to pull at him, and he didn't even look like he was exerting any strength to resist her. It was both scary and intriguing at the same time. When in control, he took the greatest care with her, but if he ever lost control, she would be in big trouble. Especially because he was immune to her touch.

"Fine. I'm leaving," Jazmine announced and turned away.

A hand grabbed her wrist.

She turned around.

Evan looked up at her with pained red eyes, the black pupil tiny amongst the crimson color. It both unsettled and saddened her because she knew he was ashamed of those eyes that were a part of him.

She squatted down in front of him and touched his face. His skin was warm and soft. He was all hard edges and smooth surfaces, and she loved the juxtaposition of that. Jazmine decided that touching someone was awesome. Her fingers sizzled with the memories of his skin whenever they were apart.

"Don't leave," he whispered. He brought her hand to his lips before sitting upright.

She leaned forward and tapped her forehead to his. "I won't. You shouldn't have let that Travis guy get under your skin. What's the deal with you two? Can you talk about it now that you've cooled off some?"

He leaned his head back on the couch. "He's just an asshole. He's everything I despise in a vampire. We have this strength, this power, and he just abuses the privilege. He's not helping. If we can't do good with these gifts, then what the hell are we here for?"

She nodded slowly, better understanding Evan's mind now. He was a bleeding heart, and it made her like him even more. "Well, if you're going to fight, make it worth it. Take it from someone who was bullied even though she can kill with her touch. It takes emotional intelligence and strength to handle things you don't like peacefully. At least that's what I read in a self-help book."

He gave her a slight smile, his red eyes crinkling. "You are a wise woman, and I'm not just saying that." He shrugged. "I mean, you're right. Violence needs to stop being my go-to. I need to take that seriously."

She gave him a curt nod with a raised brow to show her seriousness.

Evan scooted forward and suddenly scooped her into his arms onto his lap.

She yelped but didn't move away. She hadn't expected that. He'd moved her so swiftly, she felt dizzy. Vampire speed was very unsettling. "The last time I sat on someone's lap was when I was seven, and I was telling the mall Santa what I wanted for Christmas."

Evan smirked and began to rub her back. "Well, it's not Christmas, but is there anything you want?"

She swept hair from his forehead in thought. What did she want? Everything. She wanted more of his touch, his kisses. She wanted his heart. That last part scared her the most because she wasn't sure he felt the same. She looked in his eyes. She wanted to see emotion there, something that would make him more familiar to her again.

There.

Even with those alien, red eyes she was able to see emotion.

Tenderness.

"Why won't your eyes go back?" she asked.

He lost his smile. "Vampires eyes go red when they go into bloodlust, when they're fighting, when they've over-indulged in blood, and when they want to bond with someone."

Jazmine scrunched her face in thought. "A vampire bond? I read about that. Vampires can bond with each other or other beings and become mates."

Evan nodded. "Only we call our mates consorts. At least that's the term that got accepted a few years back. It's all made up."

"Do all vampires have consorts?"

He shook his head. "No. It's not necessary. A consort can make you stronger. They're also good for donations." He grew quiet and looked down at her lap. "I think there is a primal side of me that wants you as my consort. It's been that way ever since you touched me, and I tasted your blood. I've been ignoring it. I wasn't sure that's what it was, but I know now."

She gnawed the inside of her cheek in thought. There were many things she was open to, but being the consort of a vampire made her extremely nervous. If he died, she would die with him as the consort. The only benefit to her was a longer life—which she already had as a paranormal— higher healing abilities, and telepathy between the two of them.

"I'm not telling you this so that you'll be my consort. I just don't want you to be scared of me. The last thing on my mind is to hurt you." He touched her chin and moved her face gently to him, softly kissing her lips.

Zap, another bolt of amorous shock went to her core. She never told Evan, but his kiss was her first. Theo had kissed her once just to be funny one night when they'd had too much to drink. He hadn't been into her, of course, but he'd felt bad she'd never kissed anyone. It wasn't a real kiss. She knew better now. Evan's full lips on hers stole her breath. The taste of his smooth lips and the heat radiating from him felt all consuming and gave her a buzz that she enjoyed.

He moved his lips to her neck again.

She threw her head back involuntarily. "But I don't like sharing. I'm being selfish and want you just for me. Is that okay? At least for a little while," he said before moving his lips to her earlobe and flicked the skin with his tongue.

She could barely concentrate on what he was saying. Her eyes fluttered closed, and she gave a hard swallow before speaking. "Uh-huh, that's fine."

"Good," he whispered into her ear, his cool breath affecting her again. He moved his lips back down to her neck and stayed there for a while, gently sucking on the skin. She feared he might nick her with his fangs, but he had absolute control. And then a naughty thought arose. What if he had bitten her again? Would it be so bad? It certainly was enjoyable the first time.

"When was the last time you drank?" she said in a low voice. She placed a hand on his chest, and the other hand squeezed his knee for balance.

He moved inches from her neck. "I can't remember. I can be bad about that sometimes. Being blood deprived can also lead to red eyes and bloodlust so I really need to be better about that."

"It's okay if you need to bite. Just for a little bit."

He stiffened under her. "I don't want to hurt you."

She opened her eyes, looking up at the ceiling. "You didn't before. You won't now." She tilted her head farther to the side, fully exposing her neck.

There was a long pause before she soon felt his warm breath on her neck again. First, there were hot kisses and gentle sucking, but this soon gave way to just the tiniest of pinches followed swiftly by a euphoric pleasure.

Her back weakened, and Evan supported her with his hand as he continued to draw blood from her. His hand moved up to her right breast, massaging it and tweaking the nipple. She was left in sensory overload as he continued to press his lips against her soft skin and release the endorphins from his fangs into her bloodstream.

Her mouth opened in a moan, and she shocked herself from the sound. She felt momentarily embarrassed, but the noise must have affected Evan because he only pressed her closer. She felt him come alive under her, and that only increased her excitement. She wasn't sure if she was ready for anything more, but she also knew that she wanted him.

Evan suddenly retracted his fangs and pulled his mouth away from her, causing her to sigh with discontent. He licked his lips then licked the blood from her neck where the bite marks were already healing, sending another tiny pulse of excitement through her.

"Sorry, I needed to stop before I took too much. Thank you."

She looked over to him, his eyes already bleeding back to brown. "You have good self-control." She lay her head on his shoulder, feeling suddenly exhausted as he continued to stroke her back.

"It's not easy around you." He kissed the top of her head again which, although less erogenous, still delighted her.

The phone rang, and Evan groaned.

Jazmine moved off of him onto the couch, and he reached over to the side table to answer the call.

He only spoke briefly, so she couldn't get a clear idea of the conversation until Evan hung up.

"The head of the town wants to meet us for dinner tomorrow."

Jazmine frowned. Why would a town leader want to meet her? She wasn't important. "Why?"

He gave a sheepish grin. "We'll find out tomorrow."

"Shit." She caught him muttering the same under his breath.

CHAPTER 14

*E*van tried to grab Jazmine's hand that following evening, but she kept her hands shoved in the pockets of her full flower-patterned skirt. Her lips were tight, almost thin, lines.

"Why can't I hold your hand?" he asked, as he drove them to Jaspers.

"We need to stop being so touchy right now. It'll be inappropriate in front of Jasper," she replied. She looked sick, and he knew she was fighting nerves.

"He won't care." Jasper would very much care. She wasn't a vampire, and he was a snob about such things.

Jazmine side-eyed him with a frown. "You're a liar." Damn, she was smart.

"He'll get over it."

"That's not what your sister said."

He groaned. "Damn it, I knew I should have gone with you to brunch. What lies did she tell you?"

She snorted. "She told me everything. That you're a stubborn loner with too much pride and poor fashion sense. She said you never really had a girlfriend, just a bunch of hookups. Also, that Jasper wouldn't approve of me, but she would try to talk me up because she likes me."

Evan could have yelled. "Glad she likes you. She doesn't seem to like me very much, though."

Jazmine rested her head against the window. "She likes you very much, I think. She just is a shit-starter. Like any sibling would be."

Jazmine was a perceptive one. He wasn't surprised that all Thalia's unkind words hadn't run her off. Of course, she was also here on a job, so perhaps that wasn't as meaningful as he thought.

He was, however, surprised about Thalia. She hated everyone who wasn't as elite as she thought she was. Someone who was not a vampire was at the bottom with regular humans. The fact that she was seemingly taking a liking to Jazmine left him confused, but he had other things to worry about. Like dinner with his father.

"How are Paige and Theo? Did you hear from them?"

"Yup," she said, staring out of the passenger side window. "Told them all about the town and Thalia, King, and Travis."

Evan frowned. "Why mention Travis?"

She glared at him with squinted eyes. "Because I tell the whole truth to people. Just like I told them who your father was."

Evan poked his lips out in confusion. "You tell the whole truth? So, you told them that you were able to make my heart beat again?"

Jazmine closed her eyes and turned her back to him. "You got me there. I'm delaying sharing that with them, but I will say something."

Evan nodded slowly. "Well, we're here." He pulled up to a large brownstone at the end of a quiet, picturesque, residential block. Until the last two years, Evan had stayed in Jasper's four bedroom home along with Thalia, who still remained there.

Jazmine looked up at the house with wide nervous eyes, and Evan grabbed her hand to settle her. She looked down at their hands as if deciding on whether she should let him go. When she didn't say anything or move away, he took that as a good sign.

One of Jasper's guards stood at the door and let them in with a curt nod. Inside, a honey-blonde haired woman dressed in a form-fitting black dress greeted them. Yolanda Suarez, Jasper's assistant, and right hand.

She opened her arms wide and enveloped Evan in a tight hug. "It's so good to see you. It's not the same here without you," she said, her bold red lips in a wide smile.

She let Evan go and looked over to Jazmine with curious light brown colored eyes. "A pleasure," she stated, offering her hand.

Jazmine hesitantly took her hand. Evan knew that with her stenciled tattoos and thick gloves, it was okay to touch her, but he still held his breath. Killing Jasper's favorite person would not be a good start to the evening.

"I'm Yolanda. Pleasure to meet you."

"Nice to meet you as well," Jazmine replied with a soft bow of her head.

"Aww she's cute, Evie." She pointed a finger at Jazmine. "If you need anything while you're here, just ask for me. A friend of Evie's is a friend of mine." She looked back up to Evan. "Your father and Thalia are in the dining room."

"Aren't you eating with us?"

"Yes, just running off to the ladies' room," Yolanda replied before opening a door off to the right of the foyer.

"Is that your father's girlfriend? She's beautiful." Jazmine followed Evan down a short hallway to the left, pass the open stairway.

"His assistant. Although I always suspected more," Evan answered, ushering her into a room on the right just before the kitchen.

152

Jasper and Thalia were already at the dark wood table, sipping blood cocktails when they entered. Thalia smiled and gave a too cheerful wave to Jazmine, who returned the greeting.

Jasper quietly assessed Jazmine before addressing her. He rose and offered her a hand. "Evan already told us that you were unable to touch most of the living with your bare skin. I'm sorry to hear that."

Jazmine gave a polite smile and shook his hand with purple satin gloves designed with flower embroidery.

"I picked her new gloves out." Thalia exuded. "Aren't they cute?"

Evan remained silent. Personally, he preferred the simple black ones.

Jasper waved a hand to a seat closest to him, opposite Thalia, and Evan sat beside Jazmine. "Care for anything to drink? We have sangria. Without the blood, of course."

"Thank you, Mr..." Jazmine trailed off and looked to Evan with questioning eyes.

"McNamara," Jasper stated, obviously sensing her distress. "But you can call me Jasper. I know it must be confusing since Evan retained his name. Understandably. So, tell me about yourself."

Yolanda soon appeared and took a seat beside Thalia. Soon after, servants came with trays of food; steak, thick fries, and parmesan-baked broccoli. They poured Jazmine a bloodless Sangria and the others a drink from a different pitcher while Jazmine gave a high-level overview of her life. Jasper gave her cool eyes as she spoke, and Evan struggled to determine what he was thinking. Every answer she gave to his interrogation, she met with smooth ease and the ultimate politeness, yet Jasper's face gave way to neither approval nor disapproval.

As dinner wound down and the desserts were circulated, red velvet cake, Jasper turned the conversation.

He sat back in his chair, drawing a circle with his finger around the base of his glass. "You know, Evan is very important to me," he began. "I knew when we met that there was something special inside of him just waiting to emerge. He often downplays his importance, but it's my job to make sure he one day realizes that he has more to offer than just bartending. I'm sure you've witnessed his temper. It's only because he cares so much. He enjoys protecting the weak even to a fault."

Evan adjusted in his seat, already annoyed. Where was Jasper going with this little speech? Was he inferring that Jazmine was weak?

Jasper looked up at Jazmine with a small, deceptive smile. "But he can't have distractions from his greater purpose. It's bad enough that he insists on working as a bartender." He spat the last word out like it tasted awful. "I'd prefer if he joined me in running this town or at least joined the hunter force. That would fit his skill set better. He doesn't have a circle of friends despite all my efforts. He should surround himself with people who are equally focused. Elite vampires. Do you understand what I'm saying?"

Evan balled his fist on the table, ready to jump up and whisk Jasmine away from Jasper's indirect insults, but Jazmine spoke up first.

"No, I'm *not* sure I understand," she replied in a controlled tone, looking Jasper square in the eyes.

Jasper lowered his eyelids so that his smile now seemed condescending. "I'm saying, don't be a distraction from his greatness. You aren't vampire, and I can't see that you are anything particularly special to be considered elite. So, you see, there's nothing you can provide my son that would be of help to him."

"Dad, that was really harsh," Thalia stated in a low voice.

"Jasper," Yolanda said in a disapproving tone.

"I'm simply stating facts. Something tells me Jazmine is smart and mature enough to handle it."

Evan pounded the table, and Jazmine quickly covered his fist with her hand. He slumped back down and looked at her with questioning eyes, but she ignored him as she replied to Jasper. "I get that you think I'm not good enough for your son. No, I'm not an elite vampire, but I have value in this world and value to your son. He's a good person, and he's smart and caring and, yes, a protector. And if you think this speech you made was supposed to scare me off, you're wrong. I've faced a lot of fears and struggles in my life, so you don't scare me. Evan has his own mind, and if he wants to be my friend, well, I'm thankful for it. And if he decides that he's done, well, then I'm still okay because my life has been better for knowing him. And I'll shut up now."

Evan's heart ached. When was the last time that happened? He felt a literal pang of his heart. This girl. This woman had changed him. He knew it then, even if he wasn't sure he was ready to admit it, but he was falling in love with her. Jasper could suck it. Jazmine was going nowhere if he could help it.

Evan met her eyes and smiled. "You think she's nothing special, but that's where you're wrong," Evan began, addressing his father. "She's the most amazing woman I've ever met in my life. She's fearless and strong and incredibly smart. And she's beautiful and giving. And if you don't see that she's already making me better in just two weeks, then you're blind. I'm feeling purpose with her. She's made me live again, literally."

"What do you mean?" Yolanda asked in a soft voice.

He knew he was going to have to talk as soon as they saw he'd cleaned his plate. "Did anyone notice that I was eating tonight?"

Thalia rolled her eyes. "I thought you were just chewing and spiting it out in a napkin. Or you were just planning to toss it up later. You've done that before, which is so gross by the way," Thalia replied with a sneer.

Evan tilted his head with an exasperated sigh. "No, I ate my food. I can eat again, and that's because of Jazmine." He looked to Jasper. "She can't touch living things without killing them, and when she touches the undead, they're unaffected. But when she touched me, an undead vampire, my heart beat again. She brought me back to life."

Jasper frowned and looked to Jazmine. "What? How?"

Jazmine shook her head and shrugged.

Evan stood up and walked over to Jasper. "Feel my pulse."

Jasper took his wrist and pressed two fingers down. He looked up at Evan with wide eyes. Thalia jumped up and put her head to Evan's chest and then gasped when she heard the heartbeat.

Jasper looked back to Jazmine again with incredulous eyes. "Have you done this with anyone before?"

She sat up in her seat. "No, sir. I've never healed or reanimated anything."

Yolanda put a hand to her cheek with furrowed brows. "Reanimation doesn't even make one's heart beat again. This is extraordinary. So, you can breathe regularly, eat? What else?"

Evan puffed his chest out. "I'm also able to go out in the daylight and sleep like regular humans at night if I want to. But when I'm apart from her, my heart stops beating, and I'm back to being the undead. The longer I'm within a certain radius of her, the more living I become. I might have to start from scratch tonight when I go to work, and she goes back to my hotel, but I'm okay with that. I'm not just…friends with her because of what she can do for me." He said the word friend with distain. He wanted so much more with her, but without her approval, this was all he could allow himself to call her.

Jasper sat back in his seat and folded his hands underneath his chin. "I knew you were special. You must have brought out her ability to heal."

Evan shook his head, moving back to sit beside Jazmine. "No. When she went to touch dead grass, it didn't come back. It's just me she affected."

Jasper tilted his head and looked over to Jazmine with appreciation. "I'm sorry. I was so harsh earlier because I wanted to protect him. But it seems you can do more for him that I thought." He looked to Evan. "I have been spending these last several years trying to find out what it was about you that made you so special. I have a strong intuition, which is an ability that makes me an elite vampire. It's never failed, and it has always protected me." He looked back at Jazmine. "I know you mean good for my son, it's just not in the way I intended. I'm going to share something with you all that absolutely cannot leave this room. I've only told Yolanda before now. This is about Evan, and I trust everyone here cares about his well-being enough to keep this quiet?" He looked around the room, and they all nodded.

Evan frowned. What secret was Jasper holding all these years that he never shared with him and why?

"Evan, your ability to die and return as a vampire without ingesting blood first is not a simple vampiric gift. I've, thus far, heard of no other vampire who can become undead in such a manner. I've had your blood analyzed, and it was determined some time ago that you have another magic in you beyond vampirism. We suspect that it is fae, but we can't say for sure. Fae blood is hard to test for. However, whatever this other magic is, it's very powerful, and it most likely muted your vampirism and then allowed it to emerge upon death to preserve your life. It is that magic, coupled with Jazmine's that allowed your heart to beat again."

He was getting angry again, and he didn't know why. Would this knowledge have really changed his life? Perhaps

157

not, but he couldn't figure out why Jasper even cared. "Why did you keep this from me?"

"Because faeism, or whatever this magic is that you possess, is extremely rare. Fae blood is especially prized. You would have been a target, even among other vampires. There is a reason most other fae stay in their realm instead of living here on earth. It's simply not safe. In actuality, it was safer for them before the magic returned when no one believed they existed."

"So, what were you planning to do with this knowledge?" Evan sat upright, ready to bolt. He knew Jasper was power-hungry. There was no way he was keeping this knowledge from him just as protection.

Jasper sighed and dropped his shoulders. "I was hoping to develop your power and have you and Thalia help me with ruling, expand our territory even. I believe you have barely tapped into your abilities. That was very enticing to me. There are so few people I can really trust. Having a powerful inner circle is important."

Evan worked his lower jaw, anger slowly subsiding. He had so many questions about his lineage, but there was no one left alive to answer him except his missing brother. And, he supposed, it didn't matter. It didn't change his feelings for Jazmine or make him believe that she was any less special. The truth was, she was the catalyst for his change. If his father didn't accept her, Evan didn't care.

"If anyone were to find out, you'd be a target," Jasper continued with concerned eyes. He tilted his head towards Jazmine. "And so would she. Which is why you need to fall back on your fighting. You need allies, not enemies. One day someone who knows the scent or taste of fae blood will come for you, assuming that's what you are. I've already put magic on you to cover your scent, but it only works for so long, and it doesn't work well for everyone. Are you listening to me, son?"

Evan gave a quick nod and lifted a forkful of cake into his mouth. He cherished the taste of the velvety frosting and moist cake. He knew his adopted father was telling the truth, but it exhausted him. He just wanted his old quiet life at the bar. No, he wanted a life with Jazmine and no unknown magic or spells.

This wouldn't change anything. But even as he thought the words, he knew it most certainly would.

CHAPTER 15

They left Jasper's place not saying a word after dessert, which Evan insisted on eating down to the last bite. However, Jazmine's stomach was in knots. The conversation was exhausting and, quite frankly, terrifying. She couldn't even imagine not knowing fully what she was. And here, Evan had some unknown magic inside of him, possibly fae, which would lead to all sorts of concerns.

"I'm going to call out of work and stay with you tonight," Evan said as they drove back to the hotel."

"No, you need to work. I'm going to be safe alone. I'm used to being on my own inside." Jazmine patted his knee reassuringly.

"I'm sorry I dragged you into all this."

"I'm not."

He stopped the car in front of the hotel. He gave her a wide, closed-lipped smile, closing his eyes. He looked like a little kid then. It was kind of cute.

She ruffled his hair and kissed his forehead before hopping out of the car. "Have fun at work," she shouted before running towards the hotel rotating doors.

"I'm calling you throughout my shift," he called behind her.

She walked through the lobby towards the elevators. It was busy again that night. There was a popular rooftop bar in the hotel and a speakeasy in the basement. She'd never been to such establishments, and curiosity brushed at her mind briefly before she let it go. Evan was already on edge after that night's news. If he called the hotel and she didn't pick up, he'd go crazy.

"Jaz! Jazmine!" called a female voice.

It didn't sound like Thalia, her friends from last night, or Yolanda. Who else knew her there?

She spun around and raised her eyebrows in shock as she spotted Paige and Theo rushing towards her from the seating area.

"How?" she asked.

Paige cut her off. "We need to get out of here," Paige whispered, looking around.

"Let's go to my room and talk."

Paige grabbed her arm, a worried look filling her eyes. "We have to go now."

She'd never seen her sister so scared before. What was going on? "Am I in danger right now?"

"No. Not yet, but we have some information about the gang."

Jazmine sighed. "Come to my room. Let me at least get my things, and I have to tell Evan I'm going. I can't just disappear on him."

Once they got to the suite, Jazmine locked the door and turned to them. "What's going on?"

Theo spun around and then walked through the suite. "This is nice. Your boyfriend picked a good place."

"He's not her boyfriend," Paige spat. "Look, pack your things, and let's go."

"Why are you here?" Jazmine crossed her arms and stood her ground. "How'd you even get here?"

Theo walked back into the living area. "We got a witch to teleport us into town. When we're ready, we just call her to teleport us back. It's like a ride share from long ago, only no car. And she's strong enough to get us past wards. Once you emailed us the hotel you were at, we just got her to send us directly inside. Cool, right?"

Jazmine frowned, still confused. "Fascinating. Now, why are you here?"

Paige let out a dramatic sigh and looked up at the ceiling before staring back down at her sister. "Remember your attacker from *Seduction* and how he was reanimated to be interrogated?"

Jazmine nodded.

Paige pointed her finger at Theo. "Can you pack her things while we're talking?"

Theo gave her a salute. "On it, chief."

"Thanks. Anyway, I've been having some suspicions about his testimony. I wasn't in the room, so all my intel came second hand from Bryant, and I'm sure he paraphrased some things and gave me the bare minimum because it really wasn't our business. Even before sending you here, they were pretty tight-lipped. However, one thing I recall is that the guy said his group was led by a king. Apparently, he came back a little loopy, so some of his testimony made no sense. He kept saying, 'the king will be mad if I talk'. There are no monarchs here unless someone started up one, and we know this town is not ruled by a king. But then we got your email, and you mentioned Evan's boss, King. Now that makes more sense."

Jazmine put a hand to her mouth. She couldn't believe the man Evan looked up to could actually be the leader of a human trafficking group. He didn't seem like the type. Not that she knew exactly what the type was. She'd read enough crime novels and had watched enough crime shows to know that criminals weren't always obvious. However, that thought still didn't sit right with her.

"Why are the police not with you? Shouldn't they at least be in town to see Jasper, the leader? I was just at his place."

Theo rolled her small suitcase into the living area. He sucked his teeth in annoyance. "They aren't as sure as we are. They want to follow the guy around and get some proof. They said if they confront him with no proof, they'll lose any opportunity to really take him down, and so far, Jasper isn't jumping up and down to help them. He doesn't like outsiders."

Jazmine believed that. Jasper hadn't been her number one fan even by the end of the night. It was obvious he was only tolerating her because of Evan.

Paige shook her head and took out her cell phone. "Yeah, and there was no way I was leaving you here while they gathered evidence. Who knows how long that will take? And with Evan working under him, we aren't sure he isn't part of it too. I'm going to call the witch to get us out of here.

Jazmine held out her hand. "Hold up. Evan's a good guy. He doesn't know about this. We should tell him. Maybe he can help us take King down if that's the case."

Paige cut her eyes at her. "I don't trust him. He's just a horny guy who wants to get in your pants."

"If he hasn't already," Theo muttered with a chuckle.

Both sisters glared at him, and he looked away quickly, hiding his face with a hand.

"Look, I need to tell you both something," Jazmine began, wringing her hands in front of her. She then proceeded to tell them all about how she had made Evan living again. She decided to leave out the part about him possibly being part fae for now.

"Huh," Theo replied, having sat down on the couch. "I've

given you hugs, and I'm still a walking corpse. Ain't that some shit."

"So, if he loses you, he loses his life," Paige surmised. "Trafficking you wouldn't be in his best interest."

Jazmine shook her head swiftly. "So, we can use him to take King down."

Paige rubbed her temples as she began pacing the room again. "Okay, let's pull him in."

A pounding came to the door, and Jazmine jumped slightly, unnerved. Another visitor? How many people knew she was here?

Jazmine walked to the door and looked through the peephole. The female bartender from last night stood there, head down as she texted on her phone.

Jazmine opened the door a crack, keeping the chain hooked. "Hey, Rhonda, what's up?"

The woman looked up with a smile. "I just got off my shift, and Evan insisted I come by to check on you. He said he tried to call, but the line was busy."

Jazmine looked back at the phone, which was still on the hook. "I wasn't using the phone."

Rhonda gave a quick shrug. "Yeah, no surprise, our electricity and tech is pretty wonky since we only have like two tech donors here. I told him it was nothing. But you look fine, so I'm going to go." She waved her phone at her. "I'll text Evie that you're safe and sound waiting anxiously for his return." She turned and then paused. "Oh yeah, and someone else came to see you."

King appeared behind Rhonda, who moved out of the way. Jazmine's eyes widened in fear, and she slammed the door, instinctively.

Paige cursed and called their witch teleport as the door began to pound.

Theo stood up. "That door is not going to hold them," he observed, backing up.

"Shit, she's not picking up," Paige said, holding the phone to her ear.

"That's because she was told not to!" King called through the door.

Theo swore. "What? How does he have control over our witches?"

"I can answer all your questions if you just open the door!"

Jazmine threw her hands in front of her, unsure of her next steps. "No thank you. Go away now!"

She rushed to the phone and began to dial Evan's bar just as the door swung open, and a small group of vampires ran into the room.

King slowly walked in, his hands in his pocket as if he were just going on a stroll. He gave the trio a pleasant smile. "Everyone put their phones down and let's talk. I don't want to have to kill you...yet."

CHAPTER 16

*E*van poured a second round of shots to a bachelor party group and then quickly turned to prepare additional drinks for the thirsty patrons. It was their busiest night, but he just wanted to leave and be with Jazmine. When the counter calmed down for a brief moment, he pulled his phone out of his pocket to give her a call.

"Are you going to call your girl?" Travis asked, leaning on the bar counter.

Evan cursed. Why did this guy always find his way around him? He would not let Travis taunt him tonight. Instead, he ignored him and rang his room. No one picked up. Instant panic attacked his spine. Had she not gone to her room?

"I saw King, Rhonda, and some others headed in your hotel," Travis shouted over the loud music emanating from the speakers. "Maybe they were going to one of the bars, I don't know."

Evan glared at him but didn't speak, he really didn't have time for conversation. It was King's business if he wanted to hang out. Although the hotel rooftop and speakeasy didn't seem like his sort of nightlife. "Did you want something to drink?"

Travis sucked his teeth and shook his head. He looked over his shoulder and side to side as if scared there would be eavesdroppers. In fact, his whole body seemed wound up, and there was a nervousness behind his eyes. He leaned further in. "You got two minutes to talk?"

"No," Evan replied quickly.

Travis rolled his brown eyes. "Look, I don't like you, and you don't like me. That's fine. But for one moment, try not to be a total dick because I need to tell you something serious. Meet me in the back alley. Now." Travis pushed away from the bar and left.

Evan remained where he stood. This was probably a trap. He wasn't stupid. He'd go in the alley and get jumped by Travis and his gang for the other night.

Then again, there was a look in Travis' eyes Evan had never seen before. He seemed almost scared. Either he was a good actor, or something big really was going on. The nagging itch of doubt wouldn't let him ignore the possibility that there was something important Travis had to tell him.

Evan tapped on his fellow bartender's shoulder, a petite older woman with graying blond hair turned to him. "I'm about to run to the bathroom. Back in five," he said, walking from behind the bar.

Evan went down the hall of the bar, past the bathrooms and King's office until he reached the back door. He kicked it open, ready for a fight, and just saw Travis standing under a light hanging next to the door. He had his arms crossed, and he jumped slightly towards the dumpster when Evan emerged with his karate kick to the door.

What was with this guy? Why was he so jumpy? He was supposed to be the top hunter, and he looked like he was about to jump in Evan's arm at the squeak of a mouse.

"You got two minutes. Talk," Evan ordered.

Travis grimaced. "You think I don't have any morals or decency, but I have my limits. We hunt for food, and we hunt the bad guys. It's true we lock up paranormals and humans who do wrong so we can drain them of blood. But they had it coming, right?"

Evan gave a snort. "Just the bad guys?"

Travis nodded. "For me and my team, hell yeah. I don't need any negative karma on me. But we also go after rogue vampires. Obviously, we don't drink their blood because that kind of cannibalism would make us go crazy."

Now, that was new information. Not the cannibalism part but the part about going after bad vampires. He never knew Jasper cared about that type of thing.

"Only me and my team do that kind of hunting. We keep it secret under Jasper's orders."

"So, is this what you had to tell me?"

Travis let out a frustrated sigh and waved his arms in front of him. "No, man. Just let me finish. Anyway, we knew these attacks were vampire related, so we've been doing some investigating of our own. And it led us here."

Evan knew that from Jazmine's people, but he remained quiet.

Travis pointed his index finger downwards to clarify his point. "And when I say here, I mean this place. King's place. We believe he's part of this. And he has some people under him. They're stealing humans for their blood and power."

Evan frowned. "King wouldn't do that." King was like a father to him. There was no way he would be involved in something so despicable as human trafficking.

"We have proof that some of his associates are *definitely* doing it and they're going back to him. He's hosting meetings at his place with these underlings, and we got a confession from someone who worked for him. I thought you were part of it actually, but now I don't think so anymore. I heard about that attack on you both at

Seduction. You and your girl took out some of King's people. One of the guys you fought used to live here but then got kicked out by Jasper for some foul shit. But we got proof of him and King still linking up. If King is supposed to be some good guy, he wouldn't be hanging with a man like that. Trust me."

Evan shifted his stance, his mind abuzz with worry and confusion. He needed to see this proof that Travis had before he believed that King was ever behind the attacks. However, he wasn't going to naively be closed to the possibility to his detriment either. "Why are you telling me this?"

Travis scratched his scalp and quickly looked behind him as if hearing a noise Evan could not. "Because if King is behind this or at least runs the local chapter of this human trafficking ring, he might want to seek a little revenge against the woman who killed his underlings. And now's the perfect chance since she's all alone in his ter—"

Travis didn't finish his sentence. Evan had already taken off in a blinding blur of movement.

~

"Why are you here?" Paige demanded, sitting next to Jazmine.

King smiled again, pacing in front of the trio seated on the couch. "I'm just resolving a wrong. You killed my people. I can't let that go unpunished.

"What are you talking about?" Jazmine asked, trying to avoid raising her voice in fear. Inside, her mind was screaming. How the hell was she going to get out of here? She still had her gloves on, and King knew about her magic. By the time she tried to pull the gloves off, he would have snapped her neck. The only person with a chance here was Theo, but he was still out-numbered, and if they stabbed him in the brain, he wouldn't survive.

King paused, his dark eyes almost glowing as he looked down at them.

His people stood about the small space, four of them, in alert mode. Jazmine feared they would attack if she so much as sneezed.

"I had a good business going. You think running a bar is going to last me for however long we live now? And we all know the government is coming back and they'll wipe out these unaffiliated towns. The only thing that is going to prevent us from being at the bottom is capital and clout. In whatever form we can get it. I lived a hard-enough life before the world changed. This was finally my time. And my operation was giving me and my people the funds and access we need to survive for centuries to come."

Jazmine was starting to get a sense of where this was going. She shook her head, not quite believing her ears.

His face twisted in annoyance. "And then you come along. I had Evan's room magically bugged when I found out he was coming back with you. At first, I wasn't sure if I was going to do anything to you. You were Evan's girl. You didn't know any better. This is the risk we take. Evan's like a son to me. But then your sister and this zombie asshole had to fuck everything up and figure out the truth."

Theo adjusted in his seat.

Jazmine put her hand on this high. Theo wasn't the fighting type, but he wasn't a coward either. He would rush them and get killed. She would lose her best friend, and Matt would hate her forever.

King began to pace again. "Maybe if you hadn't told your government, we could've let this slide."

"They didn't believe us," Paige replied, sitting forward. Jazmine could tell she was on edge. Everyone knew their predicament. None of them could get out of the room alive if it came down to a fight. Talking was the only strategy.

King put a finger in the air with raised brows. "Ah, but they will. We're on their radar now."

Jazmine bent her fingers into claws trying to hold back her anger. It wouldn't help here. "Where are they? Where are the people you kidnapped?"

King looked over to her, a slight sorrow in his eyes. "They're gone. We don't house them."

Jazmine closed her eyes and let out a shaky breath. This man. This mentor of Evan's was a monster.

Paige cut in before Jazmine could say anything more. "What are you going to do with us?"

He pointed a finger back and forth between Paige and Theo. "I'm going to sell the both of you and kill your sister." He turned to Jazmine and sighed, putting his hands on his waist as if surveying a hopeless situation. "It can't be helped. Since no one can touch you without dying, I'll assume your blood is no good."

Theo shot up.

Jazmine pulled him back, then stood up herself. She flung her gloves off. Talking wasn't working. They were going to have to fight because there was no way she was letting those vampires sell off Paige and Theo. She'd rather they all died than be any kind of slaves.

The vampire entourage grabbed Paige and Theo in a blur of movement.

"Come any closer," King shouted, "and they'll break your sister's neck. All we really need is her blood anyway."

Jazmine stopped in her tracks, looking helplessly at her sister, who struggled against the hold of the vampires. What should she do? Her powers only worked if she could touch someone, and no one was going to get close enough for her to do any damage. Why hadn't she listened to them when they tried to get her to leave earlier? She usually considered herself to be so smart, but she insisted on staying. She didn't want to leave Evan. Her stupid heart made her an idiot.

Just then, the door swung open, and Evan appeared. He was wild-eyed with a bloodied mouth, sweat matting his hair. Jazmine could see the bottom half of a body lying on the carpeted hallway floor behind him. How had he known she was in danger?

He walked into the room, headed straight for Jazmine. One of the vampires holding her sister ran up to him, and Evan punched the man in the chest. The vampire dropped to his knees, his face going slack.

Jazmine gasped in horror as she saw Evan's outstretched hand held a bloodied heart. He tossed it to the ground, his eyes still focused on Jazmine as he continued to her. Once in front of her, he wordlessly assessed her from head to toe.

"I'm okay," she said, placing a hand on his cheek, he felt burning hot. "I'm okay."

He gave a slight, bloody faced smile that looked both horrific and heartbreaking before he turned his rage to King.

King squinted his eyes and pursed his lips in apparent deep consideration of Evan. "I think I've underestimated you, son. I never realized how strong you were. No wonder Jasper wanted you for his dynasty. We all know his daughter isn't going to do much in this world except shop. But you," he wagged a finger at him. "You took out two of my men without so much as a scratch to yourself. How did I miss your fighting capabilities? Have you been holding back all this time?"

"Let Paige and Theo go," Evan growled, stepping partially in front of Jasmine.

King tilted his head and gave a slight chuckle. "'Fraid I can't do that, son. But if you want to try to grab them, be my guest." He waved his hand and sat on top of the desk across from the couch.

Evan tilted his head from side to side and rolled back his shoulders as if stretching before an athletic competition.

Jazmine held her breath, Evan's strength was impressive,

but she wondered as well how strong and skillful he was at fighting, especially his own kind.

He then raced toward Theo. Jazmine watched in shock as Evan sped by one of the vampires holding her friend, her eyes unable to track his movements. The vampire fell dead seemingly in slow motion compared to the fast-forward blur of Evan's moves. More movement sailed to the other vampire, and Theo jumped out of the way.

Evan then sped past Jazmine, the wind generated from his movement lifting her hair up as he went to Paige's vampire. The vampire let go and Paige backed into a corner, arms against the wall as if to hold herself up.

Jazmine turned in time to see Theo struggling with the vampire, Rhonda. Evan came in to view now, having slowed to a visible pace after killing the other vampires with ease. He moved Theo aside by the shoulder before quickly snapping Rhonda's neck in yet another too fast for the eye movement. How was Evan so much faster than the other vampires? Was it due to his special blood?

"Shit," Theo cursed, moving near Paige and laying a protective arm around her shoulder.

Jazmine's older sister appeared calm in the face, but her hands were trembling fists of fear.

Jazmine decided she wasn't too far behind that feeling. She looked on at Evan, his hands and mouth more bloodied than before, his chest rising and falling at a rapid rate, and his eyes full red.

King jumped off the desk, his face somber. "I shouldn't be surprised and yet I am. Shit, vampires are fast, but you're even faster. How's that possible?" He narrowed his eyes. "Are you full vampire?"

"Let them go," Evan said in a raspy voice.

King shrugged. "No." He smiled, the corners of his eyes crinkling.

Did he find this whole thing amusing? Jazmine stood in a

room full of dead vampires, killed by a guy she was falling for who was currently covered in blood looking like a crazed killer. This was a horror movie come to life.

Evan lowered his shoulders and head, still glaring at King. He seemed almost possessed. Jazmine had never seen him so serious before. This was an Evan she did not know. "Then I'll kill you too. I don't want to, but I will."

King cracked his knuckles and nodded, still seeming too casual for the situation. Why wasn't he afraid? "Wow. She must really be something special to you for you to turn your back on *me*. Man, we could have done so much together. Oh, but don't think you'll be able to take me out so easily. See that blood serum the humans are making? Well, there's a variation that works on paranormals too, and yours truly took some. So, whatever extra you are, I can handle it." He pointed a finger. "But are you sure about this? I won't kill your girl. You can keep her. Just let me go on my way."

"I can't let you hurt people," Evan growled, his breathing slowing down.

Jazmine yanked at Evan's black T-shirt. "Let him go," she said quietly. As much faith as she now had in Evan's fighting abilities, something about the cocky way King moved gave her pause. He was older and bigger than Evan. He was also selfish. King would kill Evan if he had to in order to get out. Evan would not be so ruthless. He had heart, and King meant too much to him. Evan would fight to subdue. King would fight to kill.

"Listen to your girl. She's a smart one," King said with a roll of his shoulders.

Evan glanced down at her, his face ablaze with anger not directed at her. Between the blood, fangs, and the red eyes, she should have been scared, but she wasn't. Instead, she continued to cling to his shirt, worried.

His expression softened, but he gently removed her hands

from his shirt. "If I don't stop him, I'll never forgive myself. Is it too early to tell you I love you?"

She nodded, her eyes beginning to tear up. The emotions welling inside threatened to paralyze her. He was going to die. She knew it, and he chose this exact time to confess his feelings. The jerk. "Yes."

The right corner of his mouth lifted in a slight smile, and he gave a nod before turning away. "Thought so."

"Oh, this is going to be so bad for you." King sighed before flying towards Evan in a large blur.

Evan quickly pushed her to the side, and Jazmine tripped over the dead body of a vampire. She recovered and crawled to the doorway as she watched Evan and King claw and bite at each other against the wall over the couch, fighting in the air like angry hawks.

Theo and Paige scrambled towards her, narrowly missing Evan as he was flung across the room and crashed into the TV, cracking it.

"Let's get the hell out of here," Theo shouted, tugging at Jazmine's elbow.

She shrugged him off. "Not leaving."

"Where is everyone else?" Paige cried, looking down the hallway. "Shouldn't someone have filed a noise complaint by now?"

"We don't know what these vampires do." Theo placed a hand on Jazmine's back, and she knew he would try to snatch her out of there if things got too close. As a zombie, he was strong enough to throw both Paige and Jazmine on his shoulder and take off.

Jazmine scooted back as Evan recovered and jumped in the air before pouncing onto King, who swiped his arm out, knocking Evan into the wall. Plaster fell around him as Evan dropped to his knees, a large indentation on the wall to match the ones above the couch. Evan was even more bloody, if possible, his face now awash with not only the blood of the deceased, but his own. Jazmine could see that his nose was broken and his left eye was already swollen, though it appeared to be healing before her eyes.

The older vampire raced towards Evan before he could recover and kicked Evan in the face, sending him back on the floor. Evan spit out blood and what looked like several teeth. King then proceeded to kick Evan in the ribcage again and again.

Jazmine could barely see the vampires' movements, but she did see Evan's body rise in the air at each kick. Evan was losing, and King was going to kill him.

King reached up and grabbed Evan by the ripped collar, his body now like a rag doll. "I don't want to do this." He swung a punch in Evan's face at each word. Bloodied tears streamed down his face as he attacked. "I loved you, man. Why are you making me do this?"

"Then stop!" Jazmine shouted, moving forward, but Theo wrapped a strong arm around her waist.

"You had so much potential, but you overestimated your-self," King said through a ragged voice. "You're not as strong as me." He shook Evan, who threw lifeless jabs at King with eyes that appeared swollen shut, his lower lip equally enlarged. "You're going to get yourself killed if you keep this boy-scout attitude up. This isn't your fight. You can't save everyone. You're not Superman, son. You can break. Can't you see? I'm breaking you."

Evan shoved at him, his speed all but gone, but his will to keep fighting still present.

Why wasn't he stopping?

King grabbed at Evan's arm and bent it back, breaking it at the elbow.

Evan released a soul-piercing scream that broke Jazmine's heart. She had to help.

Jazmine turned slightly to Theo. "Toss me," she whispered.

Theo raised his eyebrows in a question.

"Toss me into King. I know what I'm doing." She really didn't. She just had hope and an idea.

Theo looked sideways to Paige, who had run down the hall halfway, knocking on doors for help. He looked back to Jazmine and stood up, holding her by the waist like she was a baby he could swing in the air. "Damn you," he grunted before tossing Jasmine.

"Give up!" King roared, hovering over Evan.

"No," Evan replied in a barely audible voice, his body in a crumpled heap on the floor.

"You dumb-ass," King spat. He grabbed Evan by the hair and tilted his head back to expose his neck. The older vampire then reared his free hand back, nails now long, sharpened talons.

Before he could slice Evan's throat, Jazmine landed on top of him, knocking King to the floor and Evan sideways. Her forehead hit the back of King's head, resulting in a momentary disorientation she also hoped would count as contact, along with her grasping his exposed arms when she tumbled on top of him. For good measure, she pushed through the pain and grabbed one of his hands.

King pushed up off the floor and flung her off his back.

She tumbled to the floor and rolled to her side, farther from King.

Theo, who was already by her side, dragged her back to the hallway.

"Is he dead?" she whispered as dizziness clouded her vision.

"He's oozing black goo from the eyes and nose," Theo observed. "Gross, now the mouth. It's like sludge. This is disgusting. Is this what your magic does? Liquify people from the inside?"

Paige rushed back, pulling at her hair. "What's wrong

with her?" her voice was practically at hysterics, and she dropped to her knees.

Theo shook his head. "Your sister decided to be a hero and save her boyfriend's life. It worked, but I think she gave herself a concussion."

"He's not my boyfriend," Jazmine muttered, scrunching her face in pain. Her head and spine felt like they were being stabbed by daggers.

Paige let out a long-suffering sigh before placing a hand on Jazmine's forehead. A soothing warmth spread across Jazmine's body, and she instantly relaxed her facial muscles as the throbbing pain in her head and back receded. "You stupid girl," her sister cried, wiping at her face with her free hand.

Jazmine looked up at Paige, her vision clear again. Yes, she'd taken a stupid chance, but being a bystander when one of her only friends was dying seemed even worse. "Thanks, sis." She turned her head and looked back in the room.

Evan was now on his knees, looking down at King, who was choking out his last few breaths of life, a pool of black goo surrounding his head and covering his face like a mask. King said something, and Evan leaned forward. Jazmine couldn't hear their exchange and decided it was not for her to know.

Evan then looked over to Jazmine, his red eyes unreadable as blood tears of his own fell, blending in with the blood already on his face. He got to his feet, still badly wounded but healing, and walked towards her.

Did he hate her now? She had killed his mentor. He had to understand she had no choice. She got to her feet with Theo's help and faced him, ready for whatever he had to say.

When he finally reached her, he grabbed her and embraced her in a one-arm hug, his other arm still broken and healing.

"I'm sorry," she cried in his shoulder, unconcerned about the blood now staining her.

"It's okay," he said, his voice hoarse.

She wanted to get out of there, to take Evan with her to the safety of her home. However, she knew that the vampires weren't going to just let them walk out of there without answering a few questions. This would not be good for the relationship between her town and this one.

"Huh," came a male voice behind them.

Jazmine and Evan turned slightly to see Bryant standing beside Paige, who gave him a tight hug. "What did I miss?" he asked, face a mask of confusion.

"King was behind the attacks. He was part of a human trafficking ring," Paige explained, forehead resting on his chest as he stroked her back.

He raised a brow, still staring at the rest of them. "Seriously? So, you were right?"

Paige nodded wordlessly.

Theo arched his back in a stretch. He was strong, but Jazmine was sure tossing her hadn't been an easy endeavor. "How'd you know to come here?"

"After you both went missing and your warning about King, it was easy to put two and two together, so I teleported to the hotel. I can't believe this," Bryant replied, a look of concern on his face as he looked down at the room full of dead vampires.

"I don't know why you're acting so surprised," Evan growled, a renewed fire in his eyes. "You're part of it, after all."

CHAPTER 17

*B*ryant's face froze, and then a look of shock spread across his face. "What are you talking about? I had no idea about this. I'm a deputy governor. I would never," he shouted, carefully moving Paige to his side.

Evan grimaced, ignoring the pangs of pain all over his face. He had several broken bones, but he could feel the itch of them repairing as he stood there. Right now, he needed to fight through the discomfort because he had more to do. "King told me before he died that you were his business partner."

Bryant snorted. "And you believe that criminal?"

"Why would he lie when he was dying?"

Bryant shrugged. "To cause confusion. That's what criminals do."

Evan tilted his head back, holding in his desire to hurt, to punch, to end the evil. "He knew about you, about the town. I never told him that. He said the *Seduction* operation was a setup. Our town leader has the gift of intuition. He can tell a lie. Should we go to him? Your town's been wanting to meet with him anyway. Well, not you, interestingly enough. Is it because you're scared you'll get found out? Or that your crime ring would get discovered and put down?"

Bryant shook his head and pointed a finger at Evan. "You have a wild imagination."

"So, it's not true?" Jazmine asked, a puzzled look on her face.

Evan rolled his eyes and shook his head.

They wouldn't believe him. King hadn't been out to cause chaos. It had never been his style. Evan recalled the many times King had helped him calm down and meditate. He'd seen King mediate on his own and walk away from confrontations. Evan was sure King had spoken the truth at his death. He'd felt it in his gut.

"Of course, it's not true," Paige spat back, but Evan caught a look of doubt flash in her eyes.

"How can you trust this vampire?" Bryant questioned, lifting a hand towards Evan. "He lied about being from here and conned his way into our town."

Evan raised an eyebrow and opened his mouth, but Jazmine spoke up. "How do you know he lied about where he was from?" She asked, eyes neutral. "When we set up the plan to send me here, we never told you the truth."

Fear shown through Bryant's eyes briefly before he composed himself. "I happened to ask someone about you when I teleported here."

"Who?" Evan asked, stepping forward. "Let me go confirm."

Bryant's upper lip lifted in a look of disdain. "I don't have time for this. Come on, Paige, let's go. I can find a way back for us." He pulled Paige by the wrist.

She stood her ground.

"I said, come on."

"Why don't we go to this Jasper?" Paige asked, looking up at her fiancé with wide eyes. "We can clear up any doubt to what King said, and we need to let him know what happed

181

anyway so that Evan doesn't get in trouble, and they don't come for Jazmine."

Bryant let go of her wrist. "Fine, stay here." He turned and started down the hall.

"If you don't stop walking, I'll make you," Jazmine shouted, outraged.

Bryant stopped and turned back to her with crazed eyes. "Are you threatening an elected official? That can be punishable by death."

Evan took a step in front of her. "She dies, you die."

Bryant looked around at the group, then back down the hallway. It was still empty. Evan wasn't surprised. It was highly possible that King had made sure the floor had been cleared.

"You all are more trouble than you're worth," Bryant stated before turning back to them, eyes now dead. "Do you know how lucrative paranormal blood is? What the regular humans are willing to offer for that access? Blood is the new currency. And currency is the only way to get power."

Evan took a step forward and hit an invisible wall. He raised his hand against the air and pressed, but he couldn't push through the shield.

Bryant snorted. "King said you were a strong vampire. I'm no fool. You're stuck where I have you."

Paige raised her hands to the sides of her face, her face a mask of frustration and sadness. "Why?" Paige asked. "You have everything."

He sneered. "Do I, my love? I am under the foot of an idiot governor. *All* these governors are just relics who want a return of the old ways. They ruined things before. This is our chance to make it right. We were children and teenagers under this new world. We were able to adapt faster. We understand this opportunity better than anyone else, and yet our elders, the old farts, refuse to relinquish control, and we just blindly follow. We need new blood. I'm not the only one who feels this way."

Paige shook her head. "You've told me this before. What does it have to do with this now?"

Evan wondered as well. He was getting anxious, standing there doing nothing as he listened to Bryant get on his political soapbox. But *this* wasn't politics. It was about right and wrong. Life or death.

Bryant looked up at the ceiling as if wondering why the others were so dense to what he was saying. "We all know the presidency will return, and when it does, the winner will be whoever is most popular. And you can only be popular if you have exposure, and you only get exposure with wealth. Same way it's always been. And I don't know about you, but I want power. I no longer want to be under a rule without being a part of who makes the rule. With our plan, I've not only grown wealth but made allies. Allies that can help get me to the top." He looked at them and then scowled. "Oh, don't look at me like that. You were never a naïve one, Paige. This world is ruthless. You've seen what this world can do."

Paige nodded with tearful eyes. "I have, which is why I would never want to add to the evil. You're trafficking innocent people. They're getting locked up and drained of their blood, used as slaves. I would never be a part of anything like that." Her voice lowered, and she wiped at her tears. "I would never *be* with anyone who was a part of something like that."

Bryant tightened his lips and sighed. "That's a shame." He lifted his hand and wiped it across his body.

Paige rose in the air and slammed against the wall. She struggled against the psychic hold unsuccessfully.

Jazmine took off in a run towards Bryant.

He pushed out with his other hand in a clawed motion.

Jazmine grabbed at her throat, her eyes wide as she gurgled out for breath against his telepathic strangulation.

"You know, Jazmine, I never liked you. I suppose you

already could tell that." Bryant turned slightly towards Theo. "If you come any closer, not only will I kill Jazmine, but I'll tear your head off before I kill her so she can see her friend die."

Theo threw his hands up in surrender and gave Jazmine a worried glance.

"Smart boy. Anyway, as I was saying. Never liked you, Jazmine. Your power is destructive. You should have been locked up and only released you in battle against our enemies. You are walking poison. A ticking bomb." He curved his fingers more.

Jazmine struggled to breathe.

Evan punched against the invisible wall again and again in hopes that this mysterious magic of his could break down Bryant's magic, his rage building. His knuckles hit the invisible surface as if they hit concrete, and the skin split and furthered bloodied his hands, but he didn't care. He wasn't going to watch her die. He wasn't going to let her die.

"The attack at the club," Bryant chuckled. "That was all my idea. I had King send those idiot vampires there, although King thought it was just for a kidnapping. I thought if I ran an operation that got us leads on the attacks, that would boost my popularity and it got rid of flunkies who I never liked. I had a feeling they'd weaken the moment the situation got too tough, and I was right. I'd kind of hoped that if they didn't get killed, they would have at least taken you, and I wouldn't have to worry about a sister-in-law who was a hazard to society ruining my future political chances."

Evan felt a split in the invisible surface, a sliver of wind that stung his wounded knuckles. He punched again, moving his hands at lightning speed, unable to even see the form of his own hands in front of him. He drilled into the psychic wall like a sledgehammer until it cracked and crumbled, allowing his arms to straighten out. He pushed his body all the way through and ran towards Bryant, slamming him to the ground.

Bryant hit the floor hard, knocked unconscious. Evan tossed his head back, preparing to tear out Bryant's throat with his teeth.

"Wait," Paige cried out, running towards them.

Jazmine fell to her knees, taking in deep breaths.

"He needs to die," Evan barked, pushing Bryant's face into the floor to expose his neck.

Paige bent down and placed her hand on Bryant's head. "I kept him knocked out," she stated. "We have to be certain before we kill a deputy governor."

"We know he was part of this," Evan shot back.

"And we have proof," Theo called from behind them. He took his phone out of his pocket and wiggled it in the air. "I recorded everything on my phone back when the vamps were trying to knock down the door."

Evan tilted his head and stared sideways at Paige. "Now, can I kill him?"

She closed her eyes, looking suddenly exhausted as she shook her head. "It's better if we just have him arrested. Let him face his crimes in front of a judge."

Could Evan allow that after what the man had nearly done to the woman he cared about? "He's too dangerous of a man. What if he finds a way out of this?"

"Let's make it so he's not that smart anymore," Jazmine said, standing up, her voice rough. "I read that the prefrontal cortex and the frontal lobes deal with cognitive abilities. Maybe if we take a piece, we could dumb him down. We could tell people that maybe it was damaged when we fought him. We can give the piece to Theo as a snack. Paige, those are the areas, right?"

Theo gave a light shrug, his chin jutted out as he considered Jazmine's suggestion. "I am bit peckish."

Paige put a hand on her forehead, dropping her jaw in

shock. "Maybe I shouldn't have forced you to stay in your apartment and just read books and surf the internet so much."

Jazmine gave her a weak smile. "I like reading."

"Medical thrillers, apparently." Paige rubbed her face and then blew out a breath, turning her head up to the ceiling as she seemingly pondered their predicament. She then looked over to Evan, looking weighted down but resigned. "How sharp are those nails?"

He looked down at his vampire talons, which grew as quickly as his incisors in battle. "Sharp enough to do some very barbaric surgery."

$\mathcal{I}$t'd been a week since they'd taken down the crime ring. Evan had stayed with Jazmine at her apartment, too anxious to leave her side. Not that he had any other place to live. His apartment was a wreck, and he'd have to hire a witch to do a cleaning and reconstruction spell if he wanted any quick repair.

However, he couldn't remain there forever. He needed to take care of a few things of his own. Upon returning to town, he'd immediately packed a few things and had headed to Jasper's place, who'd also asked him to move in, but Evan valued his independence too much now.

Jasper seemed unusually shaken after learning about the fight. Evan wasn't sure if he was more concerned with the possibility of losing his chance at a family dynasty or if he really cared about Evan's wellbeing. He chose to believe the latter for now.

Evan put a small cooler of blood bags Jasper had given him in the trunk of his car and closed it. The sound of the closing click caused a tightening in his heart. He was not good at goodbyes.

Thalia and Jasper stood at the gate in front of their

brownstone with solemn eyes. They actually appeared sad to see Evan leave.

"Is there nothing I can say to change your mind?" Jasper asked again. "I'm worried about you." He placed his hands on Evan's shoulder and looked him in the eyes as if searching for some understanding of Evan's decision.

Evan smiled and shook his head. "No need to worry. I'm going to be okay. I just need to be alone for a while and think. A lot's happened in less than a month, and I'm confused. I just need to…" He wanted to say meditate, but then he thought of King, and a pang of sadness rippled through him. "Be one with nature." That sounded stupid as hell to him, but it was all he had at the moment.

He was still having a difficult time separating the King who had been his mentor and friend with the King who had been engaged in something as horrific as human trafficking. It was causing him great frustration, and when he didn't understand things, he retreated. Even before magic had arrived, that had been his go-to move. When he couldn't fight his way out of a situation, he would run away.

Thalia stepped forward, her arms wrapped around her body. "You won't be gone long, right? You didn't pack much."

He had no idea she really cared that much. He patted her on the head, and she gave him a light swat of the arm. "I don't *need* that much stuff. I'm not like you, diva."

She stuck her tongue out and turned away, but he caught her wiping at her eyes.

"How long will you be gone?" Jasper asked.

Evan tightened his lips and shrugged. "Like I've been saying, I'm not sure. But I'm coming back."

Jasper searched his eyes with a frown. "To stay?"

"Not sure."

Jasper grabbed him by the arm and embraced him. "This is your home. Don't forget that, son. You don't have to be alone in this world. I know we aren't your biological family, but we're still your family."

Evan raised a brow. "Even if I wasn't part fae or whatever?"

"Yes," Jasper replied firmly. "This might not have started out with the most altruistic intentions, but I haven't changed my mind about this decision. Whether you decide to become a leader or not, like it or not, you're one of us. Although I do hope you come around. Maybe in this solo retreat, you'll come to your senses about your place."

Evan chuckled and slapped his back lightly. "Doubt it, but you never know."

Jasper stepped back. "Fair enough. We'll leave you to it. Don't be gone too long. Nothing is stable in this world."

Jasper gave a wave and ushered Thalia through the gates, up the steps, and into the house.

"He acts like he's really sad to see me go," Evan said aloud, looking up at the house, a mix of nostalgic emotions.

"That's because he probably is," a familiar voice stated. "And he's not the only one,"

He turned his head slightly and saw Jazmine walking over to his side. Evan tilted his head to her. "I thought you weren't going to see me off."

When he'd announced earlier that day that he had to leave for a while, Jazmine had been silent. In fact, she'd appeared to be downright unaffected. Evan couldn't lie. Her lack of response had hurt him. He'd kept waiting for her to express her real feelings about his decision, but she never did. She hadn't asked questions. Not about where he was going or how long. She'd seemed resigned. And when he'd left her apartment, she'd simply said goodbye and thanked him for his end of their deal. When he'd tried to hug her, she'd stepped back and had said the deal was over, and there would no longer be a need to touch before closing her door.

He'd waited at the door for a long moment, waiting to

hear her cry or for her to swing the door open and jump into his arms, but she hadn't. When he'd heard the TV turn on to some comedy, and then her laugh at a joke, he'd taken that as a sign and had walked away. Perhaps he had imagined that she'd felt something more for him. Maybe it'd been all about the touching experience, and with him leaving, she was done. He'd said he loved her before he fought King, but she hadn't said it back.

Jazmine shrugged and stuffed her hands in her jean's pockets. "Changed my mind."

"So, you aren't mad at me anymore?" He turned to face her.

She looked away. "Never was."

"Lie."

She glared at him. "I don't lie."

He leaned forward and looked her in the eyes, and she moved back a step, looking away from his heavy gaze. "It hurt my feelings when you didn't want to hug me goodbye."

She bit her lip. "I needed to get adjusted to not touching anyone again. Just like you have to get used to not eating and being out in the sun that much again. Which is stupid."

He smiled. "Do you want to come with me?"

She looked at him with shocked eyes, parting her lips slightly before quickly shaking her head. "Of course not."

"We could go to a cabin in the woods and live off the line."

Jazmine snorted. "Sounds lovely. But I would be a distraction. You said you have to do soul searching or something."

He nodded. She was right. She would be a distraction. He would push aside his problems and issues and focus on her. He would run her away, tiring her from his immature and violent behavior. He was still learning about himself and learning to control his confusing temper.

She, on the other hand, seemed so mature and smart. She didn't need him like he needed her. He knew he couldn't depend on Jazmine to focus his life. Even if that meant he would be undead again, he was going to have to be fine with that. Jazmine did not owe him her future. It was time he matured on his own.

She brushed hair from his forehead, a slight smile on her lips. The tiny contact that had become her habit with him, felt comforting, and his heart ached as it beat once more in her presence. "I need to stay here," she began. "Paige needs me. She's still struggling with what Bryant did, and I know she still loves him. He's sitting in a hospital now, but he's going to prison. He's not the same since we took part of his brain. I think she feels bad about that. I need to support her. She's supported me for so long. It's my time to be there for her."

He straightened, needing more of her before he left. "I know you don't need me to touch you, but can I? I don't want to make things harder for you, but I can't leave without..." He looked down at his hands, rubbing his thumbs against his fingers. "The feel of you."

Jazmine covered her face and chuckled. "You are so weird."

He grinned. "But you still like me."

She lowered her hands, and he could see tears filling her eyes. "I do. Damn it."

She opened her arms for a hug, but he grabbed her face between his hands and kissed her. At first, his touch was soft as his lips pressed against her own, and then the kiss hardened. He tugged gently at her lower lip, tasting her skin, before gliding his tongue in her mouth, wanting more of her. She wrapped her arms around his back and pressed harder to him as he explored her mouth, giving what little breath he had to her.

He didn't want to let her go. Tears flooded his eyes as he continued. His heart was full and broken at the same time. He was doing this. He was causing his own heartbreak. Yet, Evan knew it was the right thing to do. He knew himself, and he knew that he didn't want their story to end with them hating each other. If he wanted his happy ending, he was going to have to leave now.

She could touch other undead vampires. There were options for her. She was beautiful and smart, and she shouldn't have to wait for him to get his mind together. She could live a life of love without him. That thought destroyed him.

Jazmine pulled away from him slowly, and Evan felt a coldness wash over him even though it was hot and humid that evening. She brushed his cheek with a finger and looked down at the pale red, almost pink color on her finger. "Why are you crying?" She asked, still staring down at his vampire tears on her hand.

He cleared his throat. "Summer allergies."

She still didn't look up at him. "A vampire with allergies? Never heard of that."

He chuckled and walked to the driver's side of his car. "Learn something new every day." He opened the door and got in. If he paused, he would reach out for her again, and he didn't think he'd be able to let her go the next time.

He stuck his head out the window. "I'll see you again?"

She smiled and nodded, her eyes still glistening, but no tears fell.

He waved and started the car.

She waved back and kept her hand up as he drove down the street until he was no longer in viewing distance.

~

*W*hen Jasmine returned home and closed her apartment door, she walked to her living room and looked around in a daze. Evan was gone, and her world felt so much emptier now. Her apartment, her sanctuary, now felt like a prison without him.

She went to her bedroom and laid down, resting her head on the pillow Evan had used just the night before. The pillowcase still smelled of him, and she inhaled deeply, his scent sending a wave of sadness through her.

He was gone. She was alone.

In just three weeks, this man had changed her life. How had she ever been okay with her forced solitude before? Her world was so much bigger now. And yet, without him, she didn't want to experience it. She didn't care about her magic muting stencils or going around other undead vampires. She just wanted one vampire. Evan.

He had left to clear his mind, but she couldn't help but think he'd also left to escape her. She'd killed his closest friend. He had hated her on some subconscious level. He said he didn't blame her. He thanked her for saving his life, but could she really believe him? When he had asked her to come with him, was he just saying that to be polite?

But the way he'd kissed her when he'd left. It'd felt real. It'd felt good. That kiss had felt like more than a goodbye. It'd felt full of promise and love. And when she'd felt his tears on her cheek, it had almost been too much for her to bear. The red streak of his vampire's tears were shocking and yet beautiful against his tanned skin.

She had tried to be stoic. She hadn't wanted to be needy and make it hard on him. And she thought if she'd fooled herself into believing it wasn't a big thing for him to leave, it actually wouldn't hurt. She'd faked laughed at a dumb TV show when he'd left, trying to psyche her mind into feeling better, like she'd read in one of her self-help books. It hadn't worked, and her laughter had only ended up turning into crying. She was so stupid.

She looked down at her hands again, the stain from where she wiped his tears still there. She balled her fist and closed her eyes. Her chest hurt. It ached. He was gone. He was gone. She was alone.

A knock at her door roused her out of a deep abyss, and she sluggishly rose to answer it. What if it was him? What if he'd changed his mind? Maybe she should go with him. She could give him his space and let him self-reflect in the quiet of the woods while she stayed in the cabin and read books. It didn't sound so bad, actually. She would tell him yes this time.

She swung open the door, not looking through the peephole as she usually did, and her shoulders dropped when she saw Paige standing there with a covered pan. She stepped back, feeling numb, her throat painfully dry.

Paige walked through and headed to the kitchen as Jazmine closed the door behind her.

"I made a cake. Your favorite. Chocolate cake. Cake is good. Cake's been helping me all week. This is the second one I've made. I really should have shared the last one. I ate the whole damn thing. Want a sli—" Paige put the pan down on the counter and turned to see her sister standing in the kitchen entrance, sobbing.

Jazmine's cries wracked her body. Tears clouded her vision, and she cried so hard, her throat hurt. She wrapped her hands around the base of her throat as if to soothe the pain away, but it did no good. "He's gone. He's gone." She removed a hand from her throat and wrapped it across her belly.

Paige rushed to her and draped an arm around her back. "I know, honey. I'm so sorry. If it's meant to be, it will be. You're so young. *I'm* so young." She chuckled. "We both have so much more living and feeling to do. Your world has opened up, and I don't want you to close it again. I was wrong for forcing you to stay inside. No one should have to live like that. You're going to get those temporary tattoos to bind your powers, and then we're going to go out to dinner and to the bars. Flirt with guys. Go shopping. And if anyone tries anything, I will beat them up. And then I'll feel bad and heal them since that's my thing. And we'll find a way for you to control your powers. The tattoos are just a start of something good. I can feel it."

Jazmine's cries settled down until they became sniffles. She straightened and looked at her sister. She wiped at her face. "Can we go to Max's to dance? Theo says it's a lot of fun."

Paige's eyes lit up with a smile. "It is! And we can dress up and do shots. We're about to be so pedestrian."

"Like in the movies?"

Paige nodded. "Like in the movies."

Jazmine started to cry again.

"What's wrong?" Paige asked, rubbing Jazmine's back.

"I'm going clubbing with my sister," Jazmine laugh-cried. "I'm so happy."

Paige burst out in laughter, tears filling her own eyes. "We're going to be okay."

Jazmine nodded, tears still flowing but beginning to feel healed.

EPILOGUE

SIX MONTHS LATER

*J*azmine looked out of her sister's small kitchen window and frowned. Fat snowflakes fluttered lazily to the snow-covered ground. She rubbed her sweater-covered arms as a cold breeze snuck through the cracks of the window frame.

She hated the winter, and there was still another month of it to go. The dreary skies and cold apartment. It was depressing.

"Okay," Matt announced. "If you don't think this is the best old fashioned you have ever had, then you simply have no taste, and I can't be friends with you."

He passed Jazmine a short glass of brown liquid, and she took a sip. The sweet drink slid down her throat smoothly. "Delicious," she exclaimed. She looked at the glass. "Where have you been all my life."

"It's a tad too sweet," Theo stated, eyeing the drink in his hand as he smacked his lips.

Matt rolled his eyes. "We're breaking up. I date women now. Jazmine, you're my girlfriend."

"I think it's great," Paige said, walking into the kitchen from the dining area, before biting into a chip from the collection of food on the dining room table.

"Look, now I have two girlfriends. God is good," the gargoyle cracked, pointing a finger upward.

Theo shrugged. "You'll come back. I'm not worried."

Jazmine smiled at the group, feeling full. In the past six months, she had lived more than she'd ever lived before. While they hadn't found a way to help her control her magic without the tattoos, she was content with having to get them reapplied every week. It was well worth the money for her to experience life.

While most townspeople still stayed clear of her, several seemed to feel comfortable with her around after Matt had bravely allowed her to demonstrate that she was safe by touching him. She was even making friends. She kept her job in her apartment but got out whenever she could.

From time to time, she heard from Thalia, who had heard no word about Evan. Once they both realized that neither was hearing from him, their correspondence disappeared until she maintained no connection with the D.C. vampire town except for what she heard on the news, which was very limited. Jasper kept his town private, and her town remained separate ever since the trafficking scandal had come to light.

Jazmine had hopes that the towns would become allies after the shared experience but the leadership seemed to dislike each other even more, both blaming the other for negative influences.

For now, in small ways, she felt like before she had met Evan. Yes, her life was fuller with experiences now, but she hadn't touched anyone like she had with Evan. No one could come close to him, and she wasn't going to push it to happen. She had way too much life to live to be concerned about finding a new guy. Her first love might never return. For now, she was still finding herself.

Theo snuck up behind her and wrapped an arm around

her waist. "Can you do me a favor and run to my apartment and grab some dip I made? It's in the fridge."

She frowned at him. "Why can't you go?"

He pointed his thumb behind him. "Because my man and your sister are getting a little too damn cozy, and I'm not leaving them alone."

She chuckled. "Other people are coming soon."

"Gooo," he demanded.

She sighed and put her drink down on the counter. "You're being ridiculous."

He gave her a kiss on the cheek and put his keys in her hand. "Love you, bye."

She shook her head and left the apartment, already seeing two familiar faces head to Paige's apartment. They waved hello to her, not clearing the space as she passed them. It felt good to be able to pass people normally without them jumping away in fear.

When she got on the elevator, an older man with his dog just gave her a polite nod, unbothered by her presence.

"You know," the man said. "I've always wanted the opportunity to personally thank you for your role in taking out those bad guys behind those kidnappings."

She gave a slight shrug. "I'm just helping out where I can."

The elevator's doors opened, and the man stepped forward. "Well, your help made a difference. I had a student who was taken. We still haven't found him, but at least with your help, I know there's one less danger out there." He offered his hand.

She looked down at it and bit her lip before shaking his hand.

"My name's Fred. See you around, Jazmine." He winked at her and left the elevator with his dog.

He knew her name, her face. He was willing to shake her hand without hesitation. She smiled to herself, blinking back the tears. She didn't think she'd ever take for granted shaking a hand or giving a hug.

The elevator doors opened again, and she got off on Theo's floor, turning left. She walked forward and then paused, seeing long legs stretched out on the floor in front of Theo's apartment. She took hesitant steps forward and then gasped as the upper body came into view.

Evan.

His eyes were closed, and she could see that he looked slightly scruffier with a slight beard and his longer black hair pulled back in a short ponytail. He actually looked kind of hot with the change.

What should she do? Wake him up? Kiss him? Hug him? Pass out from the sheer joy of seeing his face?

She decided to tap his foot with her boot.

He grumbled but didn't open his eyes. "A simple tap on the shoulder to say excuse me works too... Jaz," he murmured, his lips turning up in a smile.

"How'd you know it was me?"

He tapped his nose.

Of course, it would be his vampire smell.

"How'd you know I would be here and not Theo?" Her voice was a soft whisper now as she tried to contain her emotion.

"I came in earlier and ran into him. He told me you were having a party. I'm not up for that right now. I wanted to get you alone. He said he'd arrange for that."

That Theo. She was going to have to kick him in the knee for tricking her. How long had Evan been sitting here just waiting for her so patiently?

She got on her knees in front of him. "Why won't you open your eyes?"

He shook his head. "I'm nervous."

She sighed, then moved forward and kissed his cheek. The contact sent her heart racing, but she contained herself and moved back. However, Evan had other plans as he reached forward and drew her back into his arms, positioning her partially on his lap.

His eyes were now open, and she could see such...love in them that it made her inhale a breath. He was still handsome, and his eyes were still kind.

"You're so beautiful," he whispered. "I missed you." He stroked her cheek with his thumb and looked over every part of her face wordlessly.

The careful attention should have made her embarrassed, but instead, she chose to relish in it, having never had a man or anyone look upon her with such intensity before.

"I am absolutely in love with you, Jazmine St. Clair. I'll never leave you again. Please forgive me."

She let out a breath she didn't realize she was holding. God, it felt good to hear him say that. "And I am completely in love with you, Evan Kitagawa."

He closed his eyes again and gave a closed-lipped smile, as if the words were an exquisite symphony to his ears.

She leaned forward and kissed his forehead. "And there's nothing to forgive. Did you find yourself?"

He nodded. "I've started to."

"Same here."

"I want us to keep finding ourselves *together*." He gave her a tight squeeze. "Because now that I have you, I don't think I'll be able to let you go."

She chuckled. "I think I'm okay with that. Where are you staying?"

"I'm still living in D.C. I can't leave Jasper behind. He's been good to me."

"Our leaders still don't like each other." She lay her head on his shoulder, a sadness threatening to interrupt their reunion. "And I know Jasper still won't think I'm good enough."

He slowly stroked her hair. "And Paige still wants to

dissect me and keep me from being a terrible influence on you. But we'll make it work. I'm not worried. You're stuck with me."

She gave him a squeeze. "I'm fine with that."

"Can we go back to your place and lay down? I just need to keep holding you for a while."

She nodded against him. The feel of him was a rewarding joy she couldn't have ever imagined.

This man whom she'd never thought she'd need or want had taught her so much about touch. And of all the forms it presented itself as, she loved the way he had touch her heart the most.

He didn't need to let her go because she wasn't going anywhere.

If you enjoyed this book, please consider leaving a review on Amazon and Goodreads. All comments help me grow as a writer!

ABOUT THE AUTHOR

C.C. is originally from Baltimore, Maryland and has actively written fiction since the age of eleven. She's an avid "chick lit" reader and urban fantasy fan. During her days, she works in Civil Rights for the federal government. In her free time, she sings karaoke, travels the globe and watches too much TV… when she's not writing, of course.

Keep up to date with C.C. at the following social media sites:

ALSO BY C. C. SOLOMON

The Mission

Paranormal World Series

Mystic Bonds, Book 1

Mystic Journeys, Book 2

Mystic Realms, Novella 2.5

Mystic Awakenings, Book 3

Mystic Memories, Novella 3.5

Mystic Souls: *Coming this Winter*

Lightning Source UK Ltd.
Milton Keynes UK
UKHW010024141220
374972UK00003B/465